BEWITCHING KITTENS

Janice Bennett
Patricia Bray
Cathleen Clare

Zebra Books
Kensington Publishing Corp.
http://www.zebrabooks.com

ZEBRA BOOKS are published by

Kensington Publishing Corp.
850 Third Avenue
New York, NY 10022

Copyright © 1998 by Kensington Publishing Corp.

''Sanctuary'' Copyright © 1998 by Janice Bennett
''Charlotte's Kitten'' Copyright © 1998 by Patricia Bray
''Lord Trevor's Tomcat'' Copyright © 1998 by Catherine A. Toothman

All rights reserved. No part of this book may be reproduced in any form or by any means without the prior written consent of the Publisher, excepting brief quotes used in reviews.

If you purchased this book without a cover you should be aware that this book is stolen property. It was reported as ''unsold and destroyed'' to the Publisher and neither the Author nor the Publisher has received any payment for this ''stripped book.''

Zebra and the Z logo Reg. U.S. Pat. & TM Off.

First Printing: October, 1998
10 9 8 7 6 5 4 3 2 1

Printed in the United States of America

BPC

THE MATCHMAKING CAT

"You are bringing that devilish beast?" Sophie exclaimed.

"Poor Harris!" the marquess said affectionately. "You would like him if you got to know him."

"I doubt it." Shooing the cat aside, Sophie settled herself in the forward facing seat. Lord Breakstone lowered himself to the seat next to Sophie.

"Are you certain that this is proper?" Sophie asked.

"It is an open carriage. What sort of mischief could we enact?"

Sophie sniffed. "You cannot blame me for being wary. Perhaps you should sit facing me."

"I will not do that! You are well chaperoned. You have your maid . . ." He grinned wickedly. "And you have Harris."

"Harris is the transgressor who caused this tangle. Do not speak to me of cats!"

"Now, now, Miss Markwell, you know you love felines." He chuckled. "How is the mother-to-be? I must make her acquaintance. Perhaps you should have brought her, to keep company with Harris."

Sophie eyed his tomcat who peered back at her with impenetrable, yellow eyes. The feline wore a red-velvet collar and leash. Such luxury in combination with his scrawny body was ludicrous.

"Where did you get that ill-favored cat?" she marveled.

"He adopted me one night, during a fearsome storm."

"Amazing." She slowly shook her head. "Gentlemen usually do not like cats. They consider them effeminate."

"I know." He languidly stroked Harris's coat. "I wonder why?"

Sophie shrugged. "I could not hazard a guess, but somehow the beasts seem to pose a threat to a gentleman's manliness. I am surprised that you dare to appear publicly with your cat."

He laughed. "I have no fears about my masculinity, Miss Markewell."

Her heart fluttered. No, he should have no worries on that score. His virility was potently obvious . . .

from LORD TREVOR'S TOMCAT, by Cathleen Clare

BOOK YOUR PLACE ON OUR WEBSITE AND MAKE THE READING CONNECTION!

We've created a customized website just for our very special readers, where you can get the inside scoop on everything that's going on with Zebra, Pinnacle and Kensington books.

When you come online, you'll have the exciting opportunity to:

• View covers of upcoming books

• Read sample chapters

• Learn about our future publishing schedule (listed by publication month *and author*)

• Find out when your favorite authors will be visiting a city near you

• Search for and order backlist books from our online catalog

• Check out author bios and background information

• Send e-mail to your favorite authors

• Meet the Kensington staff online

• Join us in weekly chats with authors, readers and other guests

• Get writing guidelines

• AND MUCH MORE!

Visit our website at
http://www.zebrabooks.com

CONTENTS

SANCTUARY

Janice Bennett

1

The light of the full moon, the Mead Moon of July, filtered through the lace curtains of the cottage, casting its soft golden glow over the furnishings. Midnight. The moon should have reached the fullness of its power. The aging Miss Sabina Dodd cast her circle of sanctuary, then stood for a long moment, arms raised, aware of the blessings of this night. Filled with a sense of an energy beyond her own, she knelt before the hearth and placed several more branches of the applewood she had so carefully cut and left to dry in secret the previous spring, for this purpose alone.

And rose petals. These she had collected at the time of each full moon throughout the spring and summer, barely opened buds still damp with the dew of early dawn. Yellow for attraction, white for purity,

and of course pink for love and red for passion. These
she scattered on the lace shawl that lay on the stones
before the fireplace. She ignited a spill and lit the
two pink candles that stood one on each side of the
cloth, then turned to the tiny black kitten which slept
blissfully in a basket beside the candle on the western
side. With the tip of a bent finger, she tickled its little
head, then laid a lodestone against its gleaming fur,
next to its heart.

The applewood shifted in the grate, and the meager
flames spurted higher, then settled. Sabina tossed a
handful of the rose petals over the burning twigs,
then added a sprinkling of elder flowers, yarrow, and
thyme. Then more rose petals, a couple at a time—
slowly, so her supply would last until the heat reduced
the branches to coals. She inhaled deeply of the
smokey-sweet incense and envisioned the love she
sought to bring to her one-time nursling and now
her charge, Lady Drusilla Aldecott.

Sabina remained on the floor, watching her small
fire, until the last of her petals and dried herbs caught
and burned, leaving only their scented ashes piled
in the hearth. She drew the kitten and lodestone from
the basket, and the furry little black ball purred as it
snuggled in her gentle hands. Here, in this kitten
that Drusilla had named Birgit and taken as her own,
Sabina centered the power.

And then, as the last glowing bit of wood faded to
blackness, it was done, the spell complete. Sabina
restored the sleeping kitten to its basket, then raked
over the dying coals to reduce the last of the
applewood, roses, and herbs to ashes. The candles

she extinguished, the cloth she folded with care, and all traces of her nocturnal workings she swept away with the broom that stood beside the hearth. The power of her circle faded, until nothing remained but the natural stillness of the cottage at Rushings Glade. Satisfied at last, Sabina carried the kitten, still in its cozy basket, up the stairs to set in Drusilla's room before seeking her own bed.

Within three months, love would come to Lady Drusilla. Sabina had no idea who the gentleman would be or in what manner he would arrive in her charge's life, but he would be the one destined to love and cherish the girl. He would come because Sabina had summoned love, and never yet had one of her spells failed to bring happiness or healing.

II

The river-polished pebbles tumbled across the black-velvet cloth. Some landed upside down; others came to rest with the carved design of an ancient rune facing uppermost. Miss Sabina Dodd drew back her hand and studied the configuration she had cast.

Lady Drusilla Aldecott stood beside the table in the sunny little parlor located at the back of the cottage. The late October sun filtered through the lace curtains, falling in a dappled design across the remnants of their nuncheon. They had cleared aside the dishes in haste after the arrival of the post.

Drusilla held in her hand one of the letters she had received, ignoring it now in her concentration on her former nurse and the prediction the little woman would utter as soon as she had interpreted the stones. Experience had given rise to Dru's faith in Sabina's readings. But experience of people, and of sporting gentlemen in particular, had given rise to her dread of the worst.

"Binny?" Dru demanded, unable to contain herself a moment longer. "What will happen to the estate?"

Sabina sat back, her expression stricken. "The new owner will bring guns and hunters. Unless we can work a miracle, he will destroy our sanctuary."

"Oh!" Dru crumpled the crisp sheet so neatly inscribed by her great-uncle's grandson and heir. "Why couldn't Cousin Robert have sold Rushings to someone else?"

Binny nudged one of the rune stones with the tip of a finger. "An estate in the forested countryside of Yorkshire? It was hardly likely to go to a London dandy."

Dru paced several steps away, avoiding the little black ball of fur that batted in kittenish delight at the flounce on her gown. "How I wish Great-Uncle Sylvester—" She broke off. What she wished, of course, was that the lovable old recluse hadn't succumbed to a seizure at the beginning of August. For decades, Great-Uncle Sylvester had preserved his estate as a sanctuary, welcoming any and all wild creatures in need of a safe home. He'd welcomed her, as well, when her father's untimely death revealed how deeply into debt that improvident nobleman had fallen. She'd been glad enough to leave London, and, with her old nurse to lend her countenance, to take up residence in the tiny cottage in Rushings Glade.

"Well," said Binny in the sensible tone she used

to bring her former nursling back to reason, "it's not to be expected he could leave the bulk of his estate away from his heir. It was good enough of him to leave the cottage and glade to you."

Dru bit back her retort. Binny was right; it would have been shocking for Great-Uncle Sylvester to have cut off his heir. And his heir, this Cousin Robert whom Dru had never so much as met, had a perfect right to dispose of his inheritance as he saw fit. But how he could have sold it to a man who would try to kill, at every opportunity, the wildlife she and her great-uncle had cherished—

"We know our answer to this, at least." She gestured toward the other letter that had been collected at the same time from the village. It lay on the edge of the table, spread open. "Not that I would have sold Rushings Glade at any rate."

Binny tilted the sheet and glanced once more at the contents. "I can see his point, though," she said, once more in that voice of reason. "The Glade does sit right in the midst of the estate."

"We will have him—whoever he is—surrounding us." Dru glared at the letter.

Binny examined the engraved letterhead. "Renfrew, Renfrew and Billingston," she murmured. "We have no end of solicitors' names. But not one clue as to the identity of their principal."

"We shall probably know all too soon." Dru turned to the mullioned window, where the crisp October breeze set the leaves shivering on their branches. Orange, now, with touches of red and gold amid the green. Samhain, All Hallow's Eve, the ancient New

Year, neared. And with it, for the rest of the county—and every other county in England, for that matter—came the season where gentlemen tramped through the glory of the autumnal woods and ruthlessly slaughtered any creature so unwise as to show itself.

Restless, she left Binny to stow away her rune stones and the kitten Birgit to tidy away the scraps remaining from their nuncheon. Wrapping a warm woolen shawl about her shoulders, she set forth for a walk. Her tiny glade she soon left behind, and found herself following the well-trodden path leading to the manor house.

A rabbit crossed the trail, in no fear of her. Ahead, a vixen drank from the tiny stream that meandered beneath the wooden footbridge. Dru paused, and the glistening animal shimmered up to her, its bush of a tail tickling across her ankle. A robin dropped to a lower branch of an aged oak and trilled a soft song in her ear. Through a break in a bramble vine, heavy with late-ripening berries, she caught a glimpse of the lovely grouse, fearless, curious birds who had never known the sound of a beater or a fowling piece.

Over one hundred acres of safety, now reduced to a single, solitary glade near the river. And the new owner wanted that, as well. He'd find there were some things money couldn't buy.

She continued along the path with the vixen keeping pace with her. A red squirrel darted from alder to beech just above her head until, on its next leap, it discovered a horsechestnut to stuff into its cheek. It scampered away to store its treasure against the coming winter.

She'd been a part of this only three short years, since the end of her first—and only—London Season. Yet her reverence for life had been with her always, fostered by her nurse. She could have been a success in London. She'd received four very flattering offers. And she'd refused every one of them, for she could not endure the never-ending boasts of these Corinthians of the foxes they had chivvied, the fish they had hooked, the rabbits or grouse or partridges they had shot.

She emerged at last onto the edge of the scythed lawn and paused under the enveloping spread of a giant maple. Beyond, past the line of rosebushes and autumn crocus lay the low, rambling manor house. Had this unknown buyer even seen it yet, she wondered. The hope stirred in her that he might fall under the spell of this magical place, that he might come to live here in peace with all wildlife—as had she, and her great-uncle before her.

The distant crunch of numerous hooves and wheels on gravel alerted her to an arrival, and she circled around the side of the house, keeping just within the line of trees. A curricle, drawn by four perfectly matched grays, swept into the circular loop. A traveling carriage and a baggage wagon already stood before the house, and a number of liveried servants busied themselves ferrying trunks and valises from the equipage through the front door.

So, the new owner had arrived already. Would he have a wife and a brood of hopeful children in tow? She hoped so; a married gentleman might well have bought an estate for the sake of his family. She even might find allies amongst them in her battle against all forms of hunting. If he were single, though, he could have only one purpose in coming to the wilds of this Yorkshire forest: to denude it of its natural inhabitants.

A diminutive tiger sprang from the curricle and made straight for the horses' heads. The gentleman who had been handling the ribbons climbed down more leisurely, his head tilted back, his gaze directed at the low, vine-covered facade of Rushings Manor. His multi-caped driving coat ruffled in the oak-scented breeze about the ankles of his top boots.

The groom spoke, a light voice with a north country accent, but only the sound of it, not his words, carried to where Drusilla stood mostly hidden by the trees. The gentleman returned some easy, joking rejoinder in a deep tone. A pleasant voice, Drusilla reflected, as the groom laughed at whatever witticism his master had directed at him. Despite his apparent lack of family, there might be hope for this gentleman.

He stood for another long minute contemplating the house, then turned slowly, his gaze sweeping the expanse of scythed lawn that encroached on the forest, then the winding drive, the hedge of yellow and red roses that lined it, the strip of lawn leading toward the clump of maples and alder where Dru stood. He stopped, and she realized with a flash of annoyance at herself that he'd seen her.

This wasn't the way she would have liked to meet her new neighbor. She could hardly pay a formal call of welcome on him, of course, but she would have preferred to allow him to at least step inside his front door before intruding herself upon his notice; it seemed only common courtesy. But already he strode toward her, and she could hardly retire now. Straightening, she fixed a welcoming smile to her face.

He moved with the easy grace of an athlete. Probably, she reflected with regret, from hours spent tramping through the countryside, shooting at anything that moved. Or possibly from hours spent in the saddle, facing his poor mount into regular raspers in his pursuit of some innocent fox. She cast a worried glance at her feet, and noted in relief that the vixen that had borne her company had slipped into the underbrush and vanished.

As the man's swinging stride brought him nearer, something familiar about it tugged at the edges of her memory. The imposing height, the set of those broad shoulders, the upward thrust of a chin she already knew would be squared and stubborn . . . She didn't need the gleam of thick waving dark hair or the deeply tanned, too-well-known features to confirm her sudden dread. Her heart plummeted toward her stomach, then flew upward to choke her. "You," she breathed.

William Dauntry, seventh Earl of Claremore, came to an abrupt halt. A startled expression flitted across his face, to be masked the next moment beneath one of polite civility. "Lady Drusilla." His deep voice held a note of amused exasperation. "This is one welcome I hardly expected. What the devil are you doing in Yorkshire?"

"Living." She managed just the one word. She

swallowed and tried again. "Surely you—you cannot have purchased Rushings, Claremore."

His wide mouth twitched into a disarming smile. "I fear I have. Does that cause you some dismay?"

She rallied, shaking off the shock at seeing him once again. "The term I should use would be somewhat stronger. *Disgust* comes to mind."

His eyebrows quirked upward. "So you made very clear when you rejected my offer. But that was three years ago. Surely we can meet now with at least the semblance of civility."

The way his hazel eyes seemed to dance had always sent a thrill through her. She turned away, hiding her reaction. "It would suit me better to meet you in London than here." Then she spun back, her despair driving caustic words to her unruly tongue. "Why did you have to come?" she demanded of him, breathless, fervent. "This is my sanctuary. You have no right to invade it!"

"I wouldn't have purchased it had I known you were here," came his frank response.

Her eyes widened. "Then you'll leave? You'll sell Rushings and go away?" It was what she wanted, what she had to want, for the sake of the estate.

His gaze rested on her, his expression unreadable. "I haven't even entered the front door, yet."

"There's no need. There's an excellent inn a bare two miles from here. On the main road. You cannot miss it. You will be quite comfortable there, I assure you. Unless, of course, you wish to travel farther. It is still quite early in the day. You may get an excellent start on your return journey."

From his pocket he drew a snuffbox, an enameled trinket depicting a scene of gentlemen riding to hounds. He started to flick it open with his thumb, then his gaze rested on it, and he stopped. "Your favorite, I believe," he commented.

Her mouth tightened. "It is no such thing, and so you know."

"As I remember, my purchasing it started our final argument."

She met his gaze directly. "I meant every word of it. A heart that can so casually deprive a creature of life must be utterly callous at its core."

"You are—and have always been—free to hold what views please you," he informed her. "I merely failed to see the need for you to express them so forcibly in the middle of the dance floor at the most crowded ball of the Season."

"Then you should not have shown me what you must have known would anger me."

"Everything angers you," came his prompt response.

"That is monstrous unfair, and so you know it. It is only cruelty I will not tolerate."

"It wasn't cruel to stage such a scene in so public a place?"

"I beg your pardon." Her words sounded stiff and insincere to her ears, which was exactly what they were. "But as you pointed out earlier, that was three years ago. The important thing is now. You will leave, will you not?"

He fingered the offending snuffbox, and regarded her through half-lidded eyes. "Do you know," he said slowly, "I don't believe I've made up my mind. If you will excuse me, Lady Dru? I wish to inspect my new house." With that, he tipped his hat to her as if she had been the merest acquaintance, turned on his heel, and strode across the drive to where his servants still carried in an amazing number of parcels and packages.

III

Dru paced the length of the tiny sitting room in a vain attempt to vent her pent-up emotion. The kitten Birgit didn't aid the process any; it danced between her feet, trying to attach itself to the hem of the merino skirts that swung so enticingly with each agitated step. "Why did it have to be *him?*" Dru demanded for perhaps the fourth time.

Binny lowered the tablecloth on which she repaired the lace trim and peered at her charge over the top of her wire-rimmed spectacles. "Unless I very much mistake the matter, you were quite besotted with the man at one time."

Dru hunched a shoulder. "Oh, when I was seventeen, and green, and indulged in a foolish fancy."

"And now you have reached the wise old age of

twenty." Binny nodded knowingly and resumed her work.

"That is not in the least what I mean!" Dru snapped. "Oh, Binny, I was quite deceived in him. He was so dashing and handsome, yet he spoke like a sensible man. And then he proved to be no better than any other gentleman." She said the last word with loathing.

Binny regarded her charge for a long moment, then lowered her gaze once more to her mending. "Of course, you explained to him in a quiet, rational manner what your great-uncle created here. And still you say he flatly refused to so much as consider maintaining Rushings as the sanctuary it has been for so long? He must, indeed, be a monster to so ignore your pleas."

Dru felt the heat rise in her cheeks. "It—it didn't come up."

"Meaning you ripped up at him, I suppose." Binny sighed.

"I'll talk to him," Dru said quickly. "I shall send Samuel with a note asking him to call." With that, she hurried to the writing desk on the far side of the room before her courage failed her.

It was not, she reflected as she dusted sand over the brief missive, that she suffered any embarrassment at her behavior of the morning. He had stirred her temper quite deliberately, and he knew all too well the inevitable results. It was the simple fact that he *could* still stir her temper, and with so little effort, that she found disturbing. He had been the most dashing of her suitors during that one London Season. She paused with the sealing wax in one hand, her gaze drifting backward into memory. Had he not been so addicted to sport—

She broke off that thought, alarmed by the touch of longing it had provoked. That, she reflected in dismay, would never do! She had made her decision more than three years ago, and her sentiments on the subject had only strengthened in the intervening time. The shock of seeing him, so unexpectedly, had unsettled her wits, that was all. If he persisted in remaining at Rushings, there need be no awkwardness attached to any chance meetings. Now that she was prepared, she could face him with equanimity.

Wrapping her shawl about her shoulders, she set forth into the garden where Samuel, the elderly man of all work, tended the autumn squash. He accepted the note, assured her it would be no trouble at all to deliver it at the manor house, but his bright, brooding eyes regarded her in speculation. Pausing only to lay aside his spade, he set forth in the direction of the shortcut Dru had herself taken earlier.

She returned indoors, hesitated in the hall, then made her way up the stairs to the cozy chamber at the back of the house that had served as her bedroom since she had come here to live. A glance in the mirror assured her that her earlier tramp through the wood had wrecked severe damage to her hair and that the hem of her gown had become muddied. Well, when encountering Claremore in the wilds of the estate, that might be quite acceptable. But she would not appear such a sad romp here in her own home.

Hastily, she stripped off her morning gown, then regarded the contents of her wardrobe with a frown. The peach-colored round gown, with its tiny puff sleeves and single flounce, had always become her. In fact, Claremore himself had complimented her once upon the way in which it set off her complexion. Not that she cared a fig for inspiring him with admiration, she assured herself. She merely wanted the certainty of knowing she looked her best to give her the confidence she needed.

She was setting the last pins in her heavy hair when an echoing knock sounded on the front door. Her hands froze, and nerves fluttered in her breast. She finished her task quickly, then rose, gave herself one last, searching study in the mirror, and hurried down the stairs. She wasn't eager to see him; it was just that it would do her no good to antagonize him by making him wait.

As she entered the sitting room, he stood before the fireplace, gazing into the flickering flames. She paused just over the threshold, studying the waving mass of his dark hair, the elegant cut of his coat of dark-green wool, the pale fawn of the buckskins that covered his muscled thighs and vanished into serviceable top boots. Perfectly at home, and perfectly attired, as always. She swallowed the sudden fear that three years of rustication had left her gauche, and strode forward. "It was good of you to come so quickly, my lord."

He turned at her words, and his broad smile flashed. "My man was making it abundantly clear I was in his way. How may I be of service to you?" He took the hand she held out to him in a warm clasp, only to release it at once.

"I wanted to apologize for this morning. Your being here took me rather by surprise."

His eyes gleamed. "I had rather thought your reaction to be horror."

"No." She seated herself in a wing-back chair and gestured for him to take the sofa opposite her. He did so, but the amused glint in his hazel eyes belied the polite formality of his expression. "You must know I have been anticipating with some dread the arrival of any new owner at Rushings."

His eyebrows rose, but he made no comment.

"This isn't easy," she said with all sincerity. "My great-uncle treated the estate as a sanctuary for all wildlife. During the fifty-three years he resided here, not one animal has ever been hunted, not one fish dragged from the river. It has been my hope that it would remain so."

"But you must have known it could not," he drawled.

Her ready temper flaring, she opened her mouth to give him a sharp retort, then closed it again firmly. She waited the moment necessary to regain control, then fixed him with an accusing eye. "You are deliberately provoking me."

He inclined his head in acknowledgement. "I find it a temptation difficult to resist. I quite enjoy the way your eyes flash when you are longing to annihilate me."

Firmly ignoring the fact that it would, indeed, be a delightful pastime, she fixed him with her eyes widened in assumed innocence. "You would know, of course, since annihilating innocent creatures seems to be an occupation dear to your heart."

"Me? An innocent creature?" He shook his head. "You are fair and far out, my girl."

"Innocent is the one thing I would not call you," she snapped back.

He beamed at her. "You always did understand me, did you not?"

"Enough to know I wanted nothing more to do with you." She rose abruptly, appalled by her rudeness, yet unwilling to take back the words. She strode away, then turned back to him. "It's useless to appeal to your better nature!"

"Quite true. I haven't got one."

Heat flushed her cheeks. "Must you always turn everything into a joke?" She drew a deep breath, then added bitterly, "I could plead with you all day, and you'd not pay heed to a single word I said."

"That would depend on whether or not I thought your pleas held validity."

"Meaning whether you happened to agree with me already." Her hands clenched. "Oh, the situation is intolerable! We cannot possibly live as neighbors."

"True. The sparks that fly between us might well start a wildfire in this precious forest of yours."

"Then you'll go?" Hope filled her. "You'll sell the estate?"

He ran a finger along the jutting line of his jaw. "With the best will in the world to do your bidding—"

She sniffed and directed a skeptical look at him.

His mouth quivered, as if he repressed a smile. "—I

fear I cannot oblige. I have a party of friends due to arrive on the morrow, and it would be quite inexcusable of me to leave them in the lurch."

"A party of *hunting* friends!" she exclaimed.

He inclined his head. "As you say. So, you must see I cannot depart, however much it pains me to disoblige you."

"You want nothing more than to do just that!" she cried. "If I had but thought to beg you to remain, then I make no doubt you would have found some excuse to depart upon the instant, only for the sake of seeing me discomfited."

His eyebrows rose. "But how could I, with my friends already well on their way?"

"Oh!" For a long moment, she simply stood, too furious to express herself.

A gleam flashed in his hazel eyes. "You must excuse me, for I have preparations to make. As always, my dear Lady Dru, it has been pure delight to be of service to you." He swept her a flourishing bow, and strode out of the room.

IV

Dru sat in the corner of the dark sitting room, hands clenched in her lap as she leaned forward, her intent gaze on her nurse. The woman knelt before the hearth, murmuring inaudible words as she poured water into the great iron cooking pot suspended over the flames. The faint glow of the waxing moon glinted off the silver candlesticks on the mantel, but only Binny's face showed clearly, flickering with the oranges and reds from the fire.

Dru opened her mouth to ask when Binny would begin, then realized she already had, that afternoon, immediately after Dru's disastrous interview with Claremore. The elderly nurse had listened with calm acceptance to Dru's blistering account of the man's infuriating pigheadedness, then simply walked into the kitchen and begun rummaging through the pantry bins for the shriveling lemons and oranges. The rest of the afternoon had passed in the methodical peeling of the fruit and the selection of herbs from the bunches that hung from the low rafters.

The soft hiss of the heating kettle reached her, drawing her from her reverie to a recollection of her own task. She picked up the bottle that rested on the occasional table at her side and resumed filling it with a variety of pins, needles, and dried rosemary. When the herbs just protruded from the top, she poured in red wine, then stoppered the jar.

"Don't spill the wax," came Binny's soft instruction. The little woman looked up from where she tossed a handful of dill into her simmering pot. "And make sure the seal is complete."

"I'm not taking any chances," Dru assured her. She turned the bottle slowly as the candle dripped red onto the glass, affixing the stopper in place. "There." She set it aside and returned her attention to Binny, who now added a handful of basil to her decoction. "There aren't many rose petals," she said suddenly. "At least, not compared with the number of herbs. Will there be enough?"

Binny murmured as she stirred the pot, then added a few of the precious petals. "I used so many of them for the love spell—" She broke off abruptly. "Well," she went on after a moment, "we do want to create an atmosphere of love, to be sure, but it's the protection we want, most of all."

"Love spell?" Dru reached down to where whiskers tickled her ankles and eased the kitten Birgit into her lap. "You never told me. Was it one of Great-Uncle's maids?"

"So long ago, now." Binny busied herself sorting the herbs, tossing in a pinch of rosemary, then one of St. John's Wort and one of tarragon. "Lemon peel—Ah, there it is."

Dru frowned. "You always remember your potions. Who—" She broke off, staring at Binny with narrowed gaze. "Binny . . ." She let her voice trail off on an accusatory note.

"I'm concentrating, dear. You know I have to concentrate." Binny hesitated, then tossed in some more dill.

"You cast one for me!" Dru accused, half vexed and half touched. "Oh, Binny, you know I have no desire—" Again, she broke off as another thought struck her. "When did you do it?" she demanded.

Binny tossed in more basil. "Oh, last July." She leaned forward and stirred with a concentration that defied further interruption.

Dru stroked the kitten's fur and was rewarded with a purr. Last July. Binny's workings always produced some result. There had been that gentleman driving through the village, but he'd been well into his middle years, and already blessed with a wife and numerous progeny. Then there had been the young and earnest clergyman who had called upon Great-Uncle Sylvester, but he had been as immune to her charms as she had been to whatever ones he might keep hidden. Then her great-uncle had died, and she had seen the solicitor who had been old enough to be her father. Then—

"Claremore!" She breathed the name with loathing. "You brought Claremore!"

Binny sat back on her heels, her expression troubled as she turned to regard Dru. "I greatly fear it's possible."

Dru hugged the kitten. "Oh, how could you get it so wrong? Yes," she continued as Binny started to interrupt. "I know I once thought I loved him. But I was wrong, and there certainly is no chance of love between us now!"

Binny nodded, her expression solemn. "And all those rose petals wasted."

"And we could certainly use them, now. Oh, if only Claremore could come to love the wildlife as do we." For a moment, that image rose in her mind, of the gentleman who had once held her heart opening his. But that would never happen, and she was a fool to let herself dream for even a moment.

"Lavender," Binny said, her eyes gleaming in the firelight. "And be a dear and fetch some marigold, will you? We'll give him every opportunity to love this estate."

"I'll bring violets, too," Dru assured her as she headed for the stored herbs. "This *must* work. It's our only hope."

V

William Dauntry, seventh Earl of Claremore, strode along the path between the thick undergrowth of dogwood and holly. Here, the tall oak and sycamore blocked the afternoon sun, and the crisp air chilled him. He hunched a shoulder in his hunting jacket and called to Dante, the giant cross-bred hunting dog who had paused to snuffle in the tangling roots of a yew.

"Not a single grouse," griped Edwin, Lord Kingley, who followed at Claremore's heels. For once, annoyance replaced the habitual drawl he affected. "Thought you said you bought this place for the birds."

"My agent found it." Claremore paused in the unexpected warmth of a clearing and listened. There *had* been birds. He'd heard them yesterday, when he'd walked over to visit Lady Dru, rustling their way through the heavy grasses, unconcerned by his passage. And there'd been rabbits, and a deer drinking from the stream. Today, the woods might be devoid of its natural inhabitants. The only living creatures he'd seen were the three gentlemen who had invited themselves for a shooting party to properly break in his acquisition.

Kingley allowed the end of his gun to rest on the leaf-carpeted path and regarded the silent woods with distaste patent on his narrow features. "Get a new agent, dear boy; that's my advice."

Claremore nodded in absent agreement. If he'd wanted to wallow in natural beauty, he'd be hard pressed to find a more perfect setting. But his friends had come to hunt. More importantly, he'd assured them of finding high sport.

The explosion of a discharging gun reverberated through the forest, to their right and considerably ahead. The giant Dante bristled, alert, but the noise grated on Claremore's ears, out of place, an unnatural, violent element in this natural setting of peace. He started forward in an angry surge, only to check the next moment as the absurdity of his instinctive reactions registered in his logical mind.

Kingley brightened. "Sounds as if Bosherston and Malham are having better luck. Shall we join them?"

"Yes." Claremore began walking again, only slower this time. Why had the gunshot disturbed him? He'd been willing enough to host this hunting party here when his friends had decided it would be just the thing. He even carried a fowling piece over his own

arm, and the hound that padded at his side he'd
carefully trained to flush out the birds, then bring
the fallen ones back to him. *So, why did it bother him?*

They'd gone barely a hundred yards when the first
angry voice reached him. A woman's voice. Lady
Dru's. His step quickened along the mossy ground.
Then a second voice, a man's, imperious and haughty,
answered the first. Apparently, Lady Dru had encountered Malham.

They stood in a grassy clearing amid the horse
chestnuts, oaks, and ash, four people in all, Malham
and Bosherston in their buckskins and hunting coats,
Lady Dru in a vastly becoming walking dress of forest
green with a brown cloak over her shoulders, fastened
at her throat with a gleaming silver brooch. She
clutched a bottle of something in her hands. Behind
her by several paces stood an older woman gowned
in purple with a cloak of darkest blue. At her feet a
large iron kettle rested on the ground.

Bosherston, an aging Corinthian whose excesses
had begun to outrun the benefits of his outdoor life,
turned as Claremore approached. "What's this
damned woman doing on your property?" he
demanded. "Startled my rabbit, right when I'd gotten
him in my sights!"

The giant hound bounded forward, tongue lolling,
to crouch at Lady Dru's feet, tail wagging as it licked
her hand. She stroked its massive head, and the fierce
animal took on an expression of besotted idiocy as
her hands absently caressed its ears.

"Really, Bosherston, your manners," Claremore

chided gently. "Kingley, come make your bow to Lady Drusilla Aldecott. You are acquainted, I believe?"

"Of course. How do you do?" Kingley gave her a quick, frowning bow. "But what the devil—I mean the deuce—are you doing out here?"

"Protecting my own," came her quick response.

"And *my* own?" Claremore inquired. That idea annoyed him. If anyone protected what was his, it should be he. Not that anything needed protecting. Why shouldn't his friends hunt his forest if they chose? After all, that was why he'd bought the estate in the first place—wasn't it?

Malham groped for his ubiquitous quizzing glass and leveled it at her with studied insolence.

Claremore's brow furrowed, his irritation increasing. "Don't be rude, Malham."

Malham's lip curled. "How should she expect us to recognize her, dear boy? She's turned herself into a veritable milkmaid. Don't see what she's doing here, anyway. A hunting lodge is no place for a female," he added in heavy disapproval. "Damned nuisance, they are, in a place like this. Some more so than others."

Lady Dru's chin rose. "Just because I have never disguised my feelings about killing?"

Malham's sneer became more pronounced. "That does make you extremely *de trop,* you know. Claremore, when you described to us in such glowing terms the amenities of your new establishment, you failed to mention the presence of Lady Drusilla."

"That was an unexpected pleasure." Even as he spoke the words, he realized they were only in part sarcastic. He did find an unexpected pleasure in her presence.

Malham snorted. "Still doesn't explain what she's doing within a hundred miles of this place. Knew she left London, of course, but don't remember anyone ever mentioning her again." His tone implied that the less heard of such an unconventional lady, the better.

"Take another ten steps forward," Lady Dru said through clenched teeth, "and you'll be on my property. And I will not tolerate your murdering ways, so be sure you stay clear. That rabbit," she added, "was on my property."

"Only game we've seen all morning," Bosherston complained.

Kingley nodded. "Same with us."

Malham, who had been staring beyond Lady Dru, frowned. "There. Grouse!" he hissed in triumph. He drew his gun toward his shoulder.

Claremore caught the barrel with his hand. "They are on the lady's property, I fear."

"Be damned to that. What the devil does she want with half-a-dozen grouse?"

"To keep them safe." Not sure whether he was amused or furious, he thrust the gun's barrel toward the ground. "She's within her rights to refuse to allow us to hunt on her land."

"That's all well and good," Bosherston complained, "but how can we possibly keep from wandering onto her property by accident?"

"I'll make my boundaries very clear," she declared.

Claremore nodded. "That's fair enough."

Malham looked pained. "To be forever on the lookout for whatever she uses as a boundary marker will quite spoil the fun of the hunt."

"What a pity," Lady Dru murmured, her smile apologetic, her eyes gleaming.

"Yes," mused Kingley, "but what I want to know is why there's game on her property and not on yours?"

"An interesting question." Claremore studied Lady Dru through narrowed eyes. His gaze touched on the small glass bottle she held, with its lid sealed in red wax. The kettle guarded by the older woman— what the devil was her name, anyway? Binny, that was it, Binny Dodd. Lady Dru's old nurse. The kettle held the dregs of a liquid of some sort. But none of it explained the absence of hunting game on his land while tiny movements among the dogwoods and blackthorn indicated a rampant wildlife only a scant ten steps away.

"Perhaps the sport will be better tomorrow," he said, his gaze remaining on Lady Dru's determined face. "Bosherston, I know you had a rather unpleasant journey with that wheel breaking. Why don't we return to the house, and Kingley may start up that faro bank he's been talking about."

Malham brightened. "I daresay I wouldn't turn down a bottle of that brandy you brought out last night."

"There's a local ale you really must try." Claremore herded them away from Lady Dru. "Start back to the house. I'll be with you in a moment."

Kingley slid his arm through Bosherston's and drew him along the path. "Pity she had to turn up here, of course," he said, "but the devil's in it she's here. Just have to make the best of it."

"Best? She's hopeless!" Bosherston declared before they moved out of tongue shot.

Claremore watched his guests retrace their steps along the path, then turned back to Lady Dru. Dante, he noted, now sat at her feet, his great head leaning against her cloak as he panted happily. "Well?" he demanded.

She opened wide, innocent eyes. "What do you mean?"

"What on earth have you done to denude my woods of game?"

A smile, quickly suppressed, tugged at her lips. "You're being absurd. How could anyone do any such thing?"

"I don't know, but somehow you've done it. What the devil's in that bottle?"

She glanced at the glass she clasped in her hands. "Nothing much. Why?" Her bright smile held triumph.

He drew a deep breath. She'd been up to something. As impossible as it seemed, she'd managed to entice the birds and small game into sanctuary.

"You will kindly inform your friends that they are not welcome anywhere near my property."

"Oh, I think you made that very clear."

She inclined her head. "As long as they are aware that any *game,* as you call it, within my glade must be treated as sacrosanct."

His eyes gleamed. She could madden him to the point of distraction, yet he would have her no other way. "Rest assured, I shall threaten them with my own direst retribution if they don't take the warning seriously. But you must mark your boundaries in a manner that they cannot possibly misunderstand."

She gave a short nod of her head. "I would build a fence, if I could."

Amusement won, and his ready smile flashed. "You manage to keep all within, even lacking a solid wall. My congratulations. I might have brought my blood-thirsty friends too near your vicinity, but I promise I will not, if under any circumstances I can help it, permit them on your very doorstep."

"Thank you." She sounded uncertain, and a guarded expression marred the brilliance of her eyes.

"In return," he went on smoothly, "all I ask is that you tell me how you accomplished this miracle." For the mystery burned at him.

A sudden, mischievous spark lit her whole face. "Why, magic, of course." Her voice dropped to the hushed whisper of a tale-teller portraying the deepest secrets of the night. "We started at dawn, sprinkling a decoction of the most powerful herbs throughout the woods, singing the animals to protection. Here—" She held up the bottle as if it were a dramatic disclosure. "—I shall bury the secrets of the moon, and with them, all power to harm what is mine." Her teasing gaze met his, and she burst out laughing. "Honestly, Claremore, you half look as if you believe me! I'll swear you just shivered." With that, she turned away, swept up the heavy iron kettle, and swung it with carefree nonchalance as she strode away.

"*Should* I believe her?" Claremore demanded of

Miss Dodd, who had turned to follow her charge. Her voice *had* made him shiver, though he'd never admit it.

Miss Dodd shook her head. "You never know what she'll be about when that hey-go-mad spirit takes her, my lord." She fixed him with a reproving eye. "You, of all men, should know her well enough to realize how fiercely loyal she can be to what she loves." The little woman held his gaze for a long moment, then hurried away.

Claremore stared at Dante. The hound rose, stretched, and trotted after Lady Dru. He had to call it three times before it returned to his side; and even then, it came with reluctance.

VI

Binny Dodd cast the last sprinklings of her decoction over the trunk of an aged oak and murmured the final words of her spell. She had worked hard that morning, starting at dawn, and her steps lagged as she turned back to the clearing where Lady Dru stood, arms raised, singing softly to summon the animals into the protected area. "They'll come on their own," she informed her charge.

Dru glanced at her over her shoulder. "I don't want to risk anything going amiss," she said, and resumed her song.

Binny opened her mouth to retort, then closed it again. Dru blamed her for Claremore's arrival, didn't trust in her spells after her bringing the earl to Rushings. Well, that was fair enough, Binny reflected. Perhaps the man had come in answer to her love spell. And perhaps it had been an error. Yet Binny had watched the encounter between her charge and the earl, and marked the nuances well. The girl flared at the man when he gave her no direct cause. And her gaze lingered on his autocratic face with a touch of longing in her eyes. As for Claremore, he'd braved the wrath of his friends to champion her position— which had been tenuous, as they had been standing on his land at the time. She also thought it significant that he had avoided meeting the girl's gaze.

A fox peeked out from beneath Dru's skirt, then vanished beneath the flounce once more. The girl started walking with careful steps back toward their glade, her shoulders slumped. "They won't all come to safety," she declared.

"But many have," Binny pointed out. "If the sport's poor enough, the gentlemen will leave, and then all will be safe again."

"Until next time." Dru stooped to shoo a lagging grouse along the path before her. The underbrush beside the trail rustled with the passage of many small, furry bodies. "Well, we shall simply do this again, and again, until there is no next time."

They continued to the glade in silence, then made their way to the edge of Dru's property closest to the manor house. There Dru collected the spade they had left leaning against the tree and dug down a mere foot in the soft, rich soil. Into this hole she placed the glass bottle she had prepared the previous evening, then stood back to allow Binny to complete the spell designed to protect the glade. Then Binny covered it up, tamped down the loose dirt, and together they headed for the cottage.

As they reached the kitchen door, Dru paused and looked back. "They certainly weren't pleased to see me, were they?"

"The gentlemen?" Binny drew her thoughts away from the animals with difficulty.

Dru ducked beneath a clump of protective herbs hanging just inside the doorway. "The London bucks don't seem to consider me acceptable. Not that I can blame them," she added with a satisfaction not untinged with chagrin. "It was never my ambition to be admired in London."

"Why should it be?" Binny forced a note of cheerfulness into her voice. "Besides, the animals admire you, and that is what's important," she added as she closed the door on an inquisitive squirrel.

"But if they cared for my opinion—Oh, what's the use of thinking of it!" Dru exclaimed. "Claremore will be swayed by his friends, for why should he value *my* views, especially when the others do not?"

"He values his word," Binny said, "and that is enough for now. Go and find Samuel, dear, and set about marking the boundaries of our glade. All will be well, you'll see."

Binny watched her charge's retreating figure, then set to work at once gathering candles and herbs for a little more magical working. It seemed her love spell might not have gone amiss after all. Yet neither

Dru nor Claremore seemed able to acknowledge their feelings for one another. Very well, then, she'd just give them that little nudge they needed to make them realize their anger stemmed from love. Smiling to herself, she called the little black kitten Birgit.

VII

The barking of dogs from somewhere just outside the bedchamber window roused Claremore. A fire crackled in the grate, bathing the darkened room in an orange-red glow, and a tinge of smoke scented the cold night air. He must have barely fallen asleep. A quick glance at the bedside clock confirmed this; the hands stood at barely ten minutes past midnight. His guests, retiring early, had sought their beds a scant hour ago.

Dante lay on the rug before the blaze, head high, ears cocked and alert. Not menacing, Claremore noted. Interested. Outside, the barking crescendoed to a baying howl of hunting hounds scenting their prey. Dante rose to his feet, muzzle twitching as he sniffed the air, and the giant animal emitted a tentative woof.

"Well, what is it?" Claremore demanded.

For answer, Dante padded to the bedside, whined with canine determination, then crossed to the door and stood with his tail wagging. When Claremore made no response, the dog whined again.

"I let you out for a run before we went to bed," Claremore informed him.

Dante merely whined again, and the tail-wagging increased to a frenzied pitch.

Claremore sighed and rose. It took him only a couple of minutes to don buckskins and coat, and he shoved his feet into a pair of slippers. Resigned to the fact his companion needed to investigate the unfamiliar noises and scents of their new establishment, he escorted the capering animal down the stairs and to the entry hall. He slid back the bolts, drew open the door, and Dante bounded outside.

Cold air wrapped about him, the gentle breeze carrying with it the damp, pungent aromas of oak, sycamore, and chestnut, and the rich decay of fallen leaves on muddied ground that bespoke the glories of autumn. While Dante stood as still as a statue, head raised, Claremore did the same, breathing in the evocative fragrances of the forest. Myriad stars canopied the sky, and through a break in the branches he caught a glimpse of a moon almost at full.

The gravel crunched beneath his feet, and he realized he was crossing the drive, headed for the wood, though he never consciously had made the decision to start walking. Still, it was a perfect night for it, and at the moment he could think of nothing he'd rather do. In fact, he *wanted* to walk, wanted to explore, wanted to find—

That brought him to a halt, but only for a moment. What could he possibly want to find at this time of night? Yet an inexplicable sense of urgency drove him on, almost as if he sought something, though he had no idea what.

Dante padded silently at his side, snuffling the ground as if he followed some scent. The baying had stopped, Claremore noted. Some night-prowling animal had ventured too close to the gamekeeper's cottage and roused the sleeping hounds. Apparently, it had gone away, now.

The thickness of the dogwood and holly kept him on a well-trodden path. Although little light penetrated through the heavy boughs, he found himself moving more quickly as he navigated over roots and around branches. Dante moved ahead, nose now in the air, ears pricked forward and tail wagging, slapping against Claremore's thigh with every stroke.

The soft, lilting notes of a song reached him, a woman's voice, a siren's call, beautiful and intriguing. He'd been following it for some time, he realized. He wanted only to reach it. Dante, it seemed, felt the same. The giant hound leapt forward and bounded along the trail.

Claremore strode as swiftly as he could through the tangling underbrush. Then the trees thinned, and ahead of him lay a clearing bathed in moonlight. As Dante raced into the open space, the song broke off. Not, Claremore realized, out of any startlement at the giant hound's precipitous arrival. The singer had simply finished her bewitching melody.

He could see her now, a dark shape stooped to the ground beside a clump of rhododendron run wild from the garden. She straightened as Dante barreled up to crouch at her feet, ears down and tail wagging in ecstatic delight. With one hand she caressed his ridiculous head; with the other she held something close to her body, beneath the enveloping folds of her dark cloak.

As Claremore stepped into the clearing, she turned to look at him, her face a pale oval, shadowed by her hood, yet shining in the moon's silken light. A trick of the stars set a sparkle in her eyes. He halted, and for a long moment he found himself unable to breathe.

"You," he said at last with incredible inadequacy. He tried again. "What are you doing out so late?"

"Birgit." She nodded with her head toward the bundle of fur she carried. Yet her gaze never left his face. "She wandered away in the dark. I was afraid for her." Her voice sounded throaty, breathless, infinitely intriguing.

"But you've found her." He spoke the commonplace words, yet couldn't rid himself of the sensation that he actually said much more, not only with his voice, but with his eyes, with a part of him he could not define.

"Just now." Her fingers stroked the kitten.

Even from where he stood, Claremore heard the purr. Dante thumped his tail in delight, and Lady Dru spoke a gentle, teasing word to the hound. The animal lay at her feet, panting in contentment.

Claremore came a step closer. "You were singing."

The moon illumined the smile that played about her full lips. "They come to my voice."

So had he. The thought drifted through his mind. The song had bewitched him. He wanted nothing more than to gaze at her, see the starlight dance in her eyes. Dance. The word brought back memories of seeing her like this before, long years ago. Slowly, unable to stop himself, he closed the space between them. With one hand, he lowered the hood to her shoulders, leaving her dark hair gleaming in the magical light. "The first time I saw you," he said, his voice sounding thick to his ears, "you were in moonlight. Do you remember?"

That smile, this time tinged with sadness, played about her lips once more. "Lady Halbridge's ball. It was so crowded and hot, I'd stepped onto a balcony to escape for a moment."

"And when I pulled back the curtain, intending to do the same, there you were. So beautiful, you took my breath away." His gaze rested on her as remembrance brought anew that wash of awareness, of awe. She experienced it, too, he'd swear she did. The old attraction welled from them both, enveloping, intensifying. Again, he could feel her gloved hand in his as he'd drawn her back into the ballroom. There'd been no need for words, no need to ask. He'd simply led her to the floor as the musicians struck the opening bars of a waltz.

So softly, he thought at first it was memory, the lilting strains filled his mind. Only it was here, now, not some trick of his imagination but Dru humming the well-remembered melody. It was the most natural thing in the world to take her hand and begin the open steps.

With the first, as she turned away from him, she stooped to set the kitten on the ground, never missing a beat. Her fingers warmed his chilled hand; or was it just looking at her again that sent the heat rushing through him? Her long hair fell in a thick braid down her back, but loose tendrils curled about her cheeks, begging him to smooth them into place. Then she stepped into his arms for the next set of steps, her one hand still in his, the other holding her cloak out as he slipped an arm about her slender waist. Her hair smelled of violets, intoxicating; then he released her, knowing in six more moves he could draw her close once more.

Beyond her shoulder, he caught a glimpse of a badger, quietly watching. Several foxes sat as if mesmerized a few paces away, and from somewhere above a tawny owl hooted its gentle cry. And there, another badger, and a horned buck flanked by two does. As Dru moved toward him once more, another owl answered the first.

His steps slowed to a halt, his arm still about her, as awareness of their unusual audience filled him. Yet the presence of these wild animals seemed only right and natural when he drew this amazing young lady into his arms. Or did he draw her into his heart once more? He felt her empathy for the forest life that gathered about them, experienced it himself.

Awed, bewitched by the magical night, he lowered his gaze once more to find Dru looking up at him. His hand that rested properly on her waist slid upward, drawing her close, as he released her fingers only to bury his own in the thick braid of her hair to capture her mouth with his. She stood in his arms, her body slight and still, but her kiss held all the pent-up yearning of the past three years. His lips brushed across her cheek, then found her closed eyes, encountering the taste of salt. Tears?

"Dru?" Her name came out half a whisper, half a caress. A tear slid down her cheek, and he caught it on his finger. Gently he pulled her against himself, the top of her head pressed against his chin as his arm encircled her shoulders. "It's all right, my lovely Dru."

"No." The words sounded choked, but she managed to turn it into a laugh. "My dearest Claremore, have you forgotten so soon? I still stand for everything you bucks and Corinthians do not. That hasn't changed. It never will."

"Dru—"

She put her finger to his lips, hushing him. "Whatever would your friends say?"

"I don't give a damn what they say."

She shook her head. "What you feel tonight may all too easily vanish with the morning light. Don't make promises or vows until you are very sure you will never regret them."

She pulled away, glanced about, then hurried to where Dante lay, head on his paws, watching. A tiny black ball of fur lay pressed against the dog's golden coat that gleamed in the creamy light. The kitten yawned as Dru scooped it up; Dante licked the sleepy feline head, then Dru's hand. She stroked the hound's ears, then without a backward glance, she slipped away into the forest. Dante followed, and the rustling in the underbrush announced that the creatures of the wood accompanied her, too.

Claremore found himself completely alone, and bereft.

VIII

Some little time passed before Claremore turned to find his way back along the tangled path. The light seemed to have vanished with Drusilla, as had every animal noise that normally filled a woodland night. The whole encounter had been magical, unreal, yet he could still feel the warmth of her body pressed against his. Except for that, it might all have been a dream.

Her presence continued to haunt him long after he climbed once more between sheets. With his eyes firmly closed, he could see her clearly, standing beneath the moon and stars, their light glowing on her hair. And he could feel her in his arms, smell again the violets mingling with the pungency of the forest, taste that tear on the softness of her cheek.

The sense of her presence lingered even in the

morning light as he dressed, arranged his hair, and made his way down the stairs to meet his guests. He'd risen late, sleeping only fitfully, waking frequently to reach for her, only to fall back groaning against the pillows as reality and reason intruded on his dreams.

He encountered Kingley in the hall, and together they made their way to the breakfast parlor. There they found Bosherston and Malham before them, seated at the mahogany table, already addressing heaping plates of beef and tankards of ale. Sunlight filled the chamber, and the strength of Claremore's dreams wavered, fading against the reality of the present.

Bosherston waved a fork of rare beef. "Shall we try the opposite direction, today? Don't want to run into that female again." He sneered the words.

Claremore stiffened. "Lady Dru—"

Malham shuddered. "Dismal female."

"No need to apologize for her," Kingley stuck in. "Not your fault she's here. Must have been a bit of a shock for you."

"It was." But apologies had been far from his mind. He'd intended to defend her. Yet these men would hear nothing good of her. He filled a plate and took a seat at the table, listening in silence as the other three discussed their hopes for the morning's shooting. They might find better sport away from her glade, he admitted to himself without enthusiasm. As their host, he knew himself obliged to assure they enjoyed themselves.

And that meant, if possible, to prevent another encounter with Dru.

Would they, he wondered, dislike her so much if she kept her views to herself? She was, he had to admit, dismayingly outspoken, ready to do battle at a moment's notice for what she believed in. If she could but hold her tongue and behave with the meekness expected of a young lady of good breeding, she might find herself forgiven her eccentricities and readmitted into the select good graces of the *ton*.

He would speak to her, convince her to see reason. And then—Possibilities, glimpsed in that moonlit glade, flooded his mind, reviving long-suppressed longings and desires.

Bosherston asked him some question, and with reluctance he relegated his pleasurable thoughts to the back of his mind and turned his full attention to his guests. The meal ended quickly, for the true business of the day beckoned. Arming themselves with their fowling pieces, the members of the shooting party ambled out into the pale, chill light of the morning. Kingley shivered and hunched his shoulders in his coat, but Malham merely yawned.

As they started across the drive in the direction chosen for that morning, an odd sensation crept over Claremore, like a finger trailing along the back of his neck. He glanced over his shoulder, but could see nothing. Still, the sensation persisted. He paused, allowing the others to move away, then turned his searching gaze on the line of yew trees at the border of the wood.

She was there, of course, more than half hidden by the shadows. She stood with hands outstretched at shoulder level; a variety of dark, wing-fluttering birds dotted her slender arms. Dante lay at her feet, his ridiculous tongue lolling from his mouth as he panted in contentment. And about the great hound, Claremore saw in amazement, scurrying even over the dratted animal's back, played four red squirrels. Then her skirts moved, and a rabbit emerged from where it nestled by her feet. Dante licked the placid creature, and it retreated.

"Good God," breathed Bosherston at his side. "The damned woman's a *witch!*" He stared at Lady Dru with an expression of revulsion on his face.

"Unnatural, certainly," agreed Malham, his sneer pronounced. "Not the sort of person one would wish living next to one, dear boy." He turned on his heel and strode to where Kingley stood waiting.

Unnatural. Claremore found himself in sudden and complete agreement with his guests. He'd even go farther and call it frightening. Yet last night he'd been enchanted by just such a vision of her as this. Now, in the cold light of morning, the moonlit clearing seemed more a dream than a memory. And very probably a bad dream, at that.

Lady Drusilla Aldecott belonged in a world of dreams. But he didn't. His friends—Bosherston, Malham, Kingley—and his usual life, those were the reality.

He called Dante, but his faithful hunting companion ignored him.

Glowering, he started forward. He wouldn't call again. If the wretched animal preferred her company—well, he'd make her a present of the faithless hound.

She stood motionless until he was a scant ten paces from her, then she raised her arms, sending her feathered companions fluttering into the nearby tree branches. Again the flounce on her skirts lifted, and this time two brown noses emerged, whiskers atwitch. A willow warbler settled on her shoulder and tugged at a strand of her glossy hair with its beak.

He stopped, exasperated. "I don't suppose you could have kept out of sight," he snapped.

Her large gray eyes rested on his face; a wistful smile tugged at her lips. "I only came to bring Dante home."

"Keep him. He prefers your company."

The hound thumped his tail, but whether at the sound of his voice or at the treat offered by his words, Claremore couldn't be certain.

Dru spoke softly, a single word Claremore didn't recognize. Dante yawned, rose, stretched, then padded over to the earl and settled at his side.

"He comes and goes only at your bidding?" Claremore demanded. "A great deal of good he'll be to me now that you've bewitched him."

Her eyebrows rose, but she said nothing. Instead, she turned to make her way back along the path. Her skirts rustled, and a number of tiny, furry feet scrambled along with her.

He opened his mouth to call her, yet what was there to say? He'd been a fool to think, even for a moment, she might fit in with society. Her differences went far beyond her outspoken views; they were part of her very being. To think he'd actually considered the possibility his friends might come to esteem Lady

Drusilla Aldecott! That was more dreaming, naught but an absurd fantasy. His friends were hardly likely to even accept her. She would never be welcome at their soirees in London, at their house parties on their estates. And any union with her would isolate him as well, not only from his circle of friends, but from his cherished position as one of society's leaders.

She'd warned him last night that the enchanted mood wouldn't last. Well, she'd been right. He grimaced and turned away. The last thing he wanted was to linger here in her presence. He wasn't afraid of her, of course. That idea he rejected utterly. He was merely contemptuous, as were they all, of the fact she chose to set herself apart from society. She could take her place among the *ton* if she wished, but she did not. That he had ever, even for a moment, considered making her his countess was absurd.

Yet every bit as much as he rejected her, he longed for her, to feel her once more pressed tight against his body.

He would sell the estate. That could be the only possible course. Kingley seemed keen enough about it, despite Dru's presence. He would speak to him that night. With luck, the deal could be struck at once. Then he could pack his bags, shake the dust of this place from his boots, and never again have to set eyes upon Lady Drusilla Aldecott.

IX

Binny looked up from the thyme she gathered in bunches to hang from the kitchen rafters to dry. Dru stood before the stove, on which a kettle of herbs and bark bubbled and steamed, but she stared into space, eyes vacant. If she remembered what she was supposed to be doing, it would be more than Binny would wager on.

"Is the decoction ready?" she asked, voice hopeful. Then, when Dru made no response, she added more loudly, "Hasn't it boiled for long enough?"

Dru started, and her gaze fell to the pot. With a soft cry, she grabbed a towel, then lifted the kettle by its wire bail from the heat. "I'm sorry. But it can't have done much harm. It hasn't gone dry."

Binny inspected the plant material floating in its dark brown stew. Tiny thyme leaves, anise seed, cherry bark, crushed mullein, all steeped together. She nodded. "Let's strain it and see how much we have."

Dru brought a crock of filtered honey from the cabinet. "I warned him how it would be." She placed her burden on the table.

Ah, so the girl was ready to talk at last. Binny had sensed her withdrawn mood from the moment she'd returned to the cottage that morning. She had had her suspicions as to the cause, but had bided her time. Now, she only said, "Men never listen, my dear."

Dru shook her head. "Oh, they listen, all right. But to the wrong people. It's his friends whose counsel and opinion he heeds. I knew, from the moment I saw him this morning, that we had lost."

Binny returned the decoction to the kettle, then poured in an equal amount of honey for the cough syrup. Dru had returned glowing from her kitten hunt the previous night with little Birgit in her arms and oblivious to the giant hound panting happily at her heels, as well as the two badgers, the ferret, and the hedgehog who tried to accompany her into the house. She'd been humming a waltz melody, a faraway look in her eyes, and she'd answered Binny's questions with an abstracted smile. That had provided Binny with all the reassurance she'd needed that her spell had worked.

Last night, at least.

Dru sank onto a chair, and a deep sigh escaped her. "I knew, of course. My way of life, everything I stand for and believe in—everything separates me from the polite world. And he's one of its leaders. I wish he had never come to Rushings."

Approaching footsteps sounded on the path, and Binny peeked through the window to see the tall, athletic figure of Claremore striding toward the little cottage, Dante leading the way. "He's here," she cried, trying to keep the satisfaction out of her voice. Dru might doubt, but here was proof that despite the opinion of his friends, the earl could not stay away from her.

"Of all times!" exclaimed Dru. She dragged off her apron, then smoothed back the tendrils of hair that had wisped into damp curls from the kettle's steam.

Binnie bustled to the front door and opened it as man and dog reached the tiny porch. Dante greeted her as a beloved benefactress, due primarily to the tasty gruel with which she had supplied him the previous night. The earl greeted her with considerably more reserve, and she showed him into the tiny parlor that Dru had just entered herself. Dante, to the hound's evident dismay, was banished by his master to wait on the porch.

Dru stepped forward, hand extended, her expression calm, her smile self-mocking. "We weren't expecting you, my lord."

He took her hand and sketched a bow over it. Releasing it at once, he strode to the window and stopped before it, staring out. "I thought it only right to come to you as soon as I had made up my mind."

Binny settled in a chair and picked up her darning. Neither of the other two paid her any heed. She wove the needle through several worn threads, then laid the stocking in her lap to study the earl's face.

Strain showed on his features, as if he had struggled long with himself over some difficult decision. Probably just what he needed, she decided; he was a gentleman to whom most things came too easily. One never developed any depth of character unless one endured one's fair share of troubles.

As for Dru, the girl stood in the center of the room, hands clasped, her gaze resting on Claremore's back. She was silent for a long moment, then her shoulders straightened. "What may we have the pleasure of doing for you, my lord?"

"Staying off my property," came his short response. He ran an unsteady hand through his magnificent head of dark hair, and he turned his head to look at Dru, his expression rueful. "I didn't mean it quite like that."

"Did you not?" Dru's voice sounded brittle.

"I've decided to do as you suggested. I'm going to sell Rushings."

Dru blinked. "I—I see. And you don't want me traipsing around the forest, interfering with the hunting trips of potential buyers."

Binny's gaze narrowed. Rather, she guessed, he didn't want Dru where he might see her at any time and thus be reminded of his conflicting feelings. Never, she guessed, had he been so torn as he was between the desires of his heart and head.

He neither confirmed nor denied Dru's statement. He said merely, "I will be leaving the day after tomorrow. My friends have decided to journey to Scotland in search of better sport. I will accompany them."

"And you won't return." Only the slightest catch

in Dru's voice betrayed the pain his words caused her.

"No." The single syllable fell on the air, heavy and uncompromising, a finality. "My agent will handle the sale. You need not be bothered with my presence any longer." Without so much as another glance at her, he turned and strode from the room. A moment later, the front door closed, softly but firmly.

Dru sank onto a chair, staring out the sitting room's window. Her eyes misted, but she said nothing.

"Well." Binny deposited her mending in the basket beside her chair and rose. "That should protect the animals for a little longer. Tomorrow is Samhain; and the day after, the New Year. Let's see what that brings, shall we?"

"It brings Claremore's departure." Dru's voice sounded hollow.

"Child," said Binny softly. "One never knows what the New Year will bring. Now come, we have the cough syrup to finish, and poor old Mrs. Dinsmore has need of a bottle. You may take it to her if you wish, but hurry back. We have much to clean and prepare before tomorrow night. We must complete the business of this old year, so we may start the new afresh."

Dru roused and accompanied her back to the kitchen. Let the girl busy herself with the herbs and remedies and the innumerable details to make their Samhain complete. Binny had plans of her own, to make it a truly magical night.

Claremore had chosen to reject Dru. Yet the decision had not made him happy. It wasn't easy to go against one's friends and one's society. It wasn't easy to be one's own person when everyone else demanded conformity. The polite world hailed the earl as a leader because he *followed* society's dictates. Yet in his heart, he was a leader. Binny, who saw more clearly than most, sensed that. He had to be, or he could not be the man for Dru.

Yet he rejected the girl, clinging instead to the approval of society.

He was afraid to take the stand, as had Dru, for what he believed in.

She couldn't influence Claremore directly, Binny reflected with a momentary wistfulness, but she could provide the situation in which he might see his own feelings clearly and make his own choice. Smiling grimly to herself, she set to work.

X

Rain began during the night, a light, misting drizzle that increased to a steady downpour with the coming of morning. Claremore stood at the window of his bedchamber, regarding it with a measure of relief. His friends would not want to venture forth with their guns as long as this kept up. From the look of the dark clouds, it was not likely to stop before nightfall. That meant there'd be no chance of encountering Dru this day. He ignored the pang of longing caused by this thought. He'd made his decision. No good would come from indulging in fruitless regrets.

His houseguests, after one glance at the sheeting rain, declared themselves more than content to spend the day playing at various games of cards. As the house boasted an excellent billiards table, this, too, helped pass the time. A pre-nuncheon raid on the wine cellars provided all the excitement the gentleman desired, and they settled down to sample the choicest of the bottles they had discovered.

The storm only increased in its driving power as the afternoon waned. Claremore tossed another log on the fire in the drawing room where the card tables had held them for most of the day, then went to the window. Outside, the wind howled through the forest, whipping the sheeting rain, sounding more like voices calling from beyond the next world.

And why not? This was All Hallow's Eve, the night when the veil between the worlds thinned and spirits could cross back and forth. Samhain, Dru would call it. The ancient New Year. A time of endings—and new beginnings.

He forced his thoughts from Dru, but they returned with maddening single-mindedness. Despite the screaming of the wind, this night would hold no terrors for her; she lived too closely with nature to be disturbed by a storm. It was the unnatural thunderings and ravings of mankind that dismayed her.

His guests reached a stage of cheerful inebriation well before dinner, and at an unexpectedly early hour that evening, he was able to usher them up the stairs to their bedchambers. He could discover in himself no desire to follow them. Instead, he picked up his chamberstick and strolled through the darkened rooms, looking at all he intended to leave on the morrow.

It wasn't a large house, boasting no more than six bedchambers, a single drawing room, and only two salons. The library afforded more comfort than space.

In fact, if he kindled a fire in the stone hearth, this might well be his favorite room.

Except he was leaving in the morning. He was selling Rushings, and would never come back.

Someone had laid a fire in the grate, he noted, and left a pile of logs and faggots at its side. On impulse, he held his candle to the dried moss and twigs, and tiny tongues of flame burst into life. With the contented crackling of the growing blaze at his back, he strode to the window and stared out into the blackness of the storm. The wind lashed the never-ceasing rain against the diamond-shaped panes, closing him into his cocoon of warmth and light. A terrible night, one in which no living creature should be out. Were Dru's beloved animals safe and in shelter? Snug in their dens, as he in his?

And would the new owner of Rushings yield to Dru's pleas to keep the estate a sanctuary?

A light blinked, somewhere deep in the trees, then again, a little distance from where it had first shone. A lantern, he realized, being carried through the forest. Dru.

He never questioned that certainty. If someone braved this storm, it would be Dru. Without a doubt, it would be the distress of some poor animal that brought her out on such a night. Exasperated, he went in search of his greatcoat.

Armed with a lantern of his own, he set forth across the gravelled drive, his head bent against the whipping rain that stung his face. An eerie crack rent the night, and at the edge of the forest a branch tore from an elm, crashing to the ground. And Dru, Claremore reflected, wandered alone and vulnerable beneath a canopy of trees, every one of them capable of dropping limbs on her. He increased his pace. Once he'd rescued her, and seen her to safety, he intended to give her the rarest trimming of her life.

He could no longer see her light. Stopping to listen intently proved no help, either; the howling of the wind drowned out any other sound. If she had fallen or her light been extinguished—He raised one arm to shelter his eyes from the torrent of rain and searched for the path that would lead him, eventually, to her tiny glade.

His greatcoat proved little protection from the raging elements. Water ran down the back of his neck, and he doubted he wore a single stitch that wasn't drenched. As the cold seeped through him, freezing even his gloved fingers and booted feet, he decided to dispense with giving her a scold. He'd just strangle her.

Lightning flashed, and thunder rumbled less than a second later. Over the raging wind came an ominous crack, followed by a thudding crash as another branch struck the ground. He glanced around, searching for Dru's light, and realized he had no idea where he was, or even in which direction he walked. Yet somehow he had to find Dru, before any harm came to her.

Then another sound reached him, faint but plaintive, a feline cry of fear. A kitten's cry. That damned, black kitten of Dru's. It had gotten lost, and that was what had brought her out.

The cry came again, from somewhere to his left. He forced his way off the path, trudging through mud, as leaves and twigs clung to his sodden coat. With the third cry, he found it, the little black nose just peeping out from beneath a bush, the flickering light reflecting from its wide eyes.

"Birgit," he called softly, and held out his hand.

The drenched bundle of fur hunkered down, then bolted away into the forest. Abruptly it paused at the edge of the circle of light from the lantern, looking back at him. Claremore followed several paces, but before he could reach it, the kitten darted away again. It could be as much of a nuisance as Dru, he reflected, and set off again in pursuit.

Once, he almost managed to grasp the aggravating kitten. Most of the time, it kept just beyond his reach. He swore steadily for several minutes, which only seemed to drive the kitten farther from him. With an effort, he switched his tone to one of gentle coaxing.

Then another voice reached him, clear and lilting, raised in a song that set his heart racing. The kitten scampered toward it. He ran, too, he realized, stumbling after Birgit, yet no longer pursuing the kitten as much as he was drawn by Dru's singing.

He forged through a pair of closely growing dogwoods and broke into a small clearing. The next moment, Dru's slender, cloaked figure emerged through the underbrush from the opposite side. The thick bush of a fox's tail protruded from beneath her mud-splattered hem, and a bright, pointed face just peeked out from a heavy fold that engulfed the crook of her arm. The kitten dove beneath her skirts, and she dropped to her knees and gathered it into her free arm. Tears mingled with the rain that streamed down her face.

Claremore stopped in his tracks, awed by the compassion and tenderness that emanated from her, wrapping about him like a warm, protective blanket. No wonder the wild creatures sought her company. Anyone must who was touched by such generous and unstinting love. He could only wonder how—and why—he had resisted so long.

The barriers, which he had tried so hard to construct about his heart, crumbled. Weird and uncanny he'd thought her, and so she was, at one with all nature, joyful and free.

Loving her, he realized, was only a small part of what he wanted—no, needed. Desperately he desired that she love him, too, with that all-encompassing, all-healing passion that radiated from her.

But would she extend it to him? Fear that he might lose her—might already have done so—washed through him, leaving him with a sick, aching dread. She was too precious to let slip away. Life without her would be empty, meaningless. London held nothing he wanted, now. Her forest sanctuary offered far more appeal than anything he could ever hope to find in the elegant salons of the *ton*. In Dru, he had found his own sanctuary.

He would fight to keep her.

He sank to his knees on the sodden ground before her. Her misty gaze met his, and a smile trembled on her lips. Hope surged through him. He reached for her, but she held him back. For a moment his fears returned, then he saw she merely shifted the fox she cradled in her arm. He caught a glimpse of one of its front legs, wrapped in a bit of cloth tinged red with its blood. Of course she would protect an injured animal.

Again he reached for her, and this time he succeeded in wrapping his arm about her shoulders. His pulse raced and his heart caught in his throat as she allowed him to draw her close.

An indignant mew sounded, and a shaky laugh escaped Dru. "We're forgetting Birgit."

"Poor thing. Here." He eased the purring bundle of damp fur from Dru's protective arm and placed it on her lap. "You came out to find her, didn't you?"

Dru nodded. "I can't imagine how she came so far."

"To bring you to me, perhaps?" He dared to smooth a strand of drenched hair back from her eyes.

She swallowed, but made no move to pull away from him. "Why would she do that?"

"Because you belong with me." He spoke with a fervency that would have startled him only an hour before.

She shook her head, and anguish showed in her eyes. "I belong here."

He felt a tug at his leg and looked down to see the other fox, the one that had hidden in her skirts, making a determined foray into his lap. He eyed it with a consternation not unmingled with pleasure. "It seems possible I may belong here, too," he said. With a tentative hand, he touched the reddish fur as the animal nudged at the opening of his greatcoat, seeking shelter within it.

"You realize what belonging here means, don't

you?'' Her wrist turned so her hand clasped his forearm. ''What you'd be giving up? You'd be shunned by your friends, you'd—''

''I'd be giving up nothing that matters.'' As he said the words, he knew he meant them. The nudging continued as the fox tried to wedge its way through the gap offered between two of the large buttons. ''Perhaps we can hold non-shooting parties here, and start a fashion among the *ton* for merely admiring the wildlife.''

''Non-shooting parties?'' Hope brightened her eyes.

''Non,'' he confirmed. ''No one will ever hunt this land again.''

''You mean that.'' Wonder sounded in her voice.

His mouth twisted into a rueful smile. ''This is my sanctuary, too. *Our* sanctuary, if you'll let me share it with you.''

She looked up, eyes wide and blinking in the beating rain that streamed down her face. ''There's nothing I want more.''

With a soft exclamation of triumph, he bent, his mouth seeking hers. The warmth of her breath brushed his chilled face, and her lips, soft as velvet, touched his. The next moment, they pulled away, to be replaced by something moist and rough rasping at his chin.

He peered down and found himself nose to nose with the nuzzling fox. Gently but firmly, he set it aside. ''Will this happen every time I try to kiss you?'' he demanded, half exasperated, half laughing as he again pushed the persistent animal down.

''Very probably. Do you mind?'' No trace of apology

showed in her eyes as she removed a drenched-but-interested ferret from his knee.

"They may come to our wedding," he assured her, eying a badger that trundled eagerly toward them, "but that is where I draw the line. There is only one lovely creature I want in my bed." He drew her close, and this time succeeded in kissing her with a thoroughness that left him aching for more.

"I don't see how we can possibly keep them all out," she warned as his lips roamed from her mouth to her throat. She disentangled one arm from where it had crept about his neck and spread her cloak to provide more shelter for the multitude of animals that scurried to her from the rain-beaten bushes.

"Then I suppose I shall have to get a larger bed." He pulled her to her feet, opening his greatcoat to wrap about her. He pulled her close, kissing her again, only to have to release her at once as something scrambled across his booted foot. He looked down to see a rounded, quilled back, fronted by a pointed nose. "No," he declared. "Absolutely not."

"Not what?" she asked, the innocence of her expression belied by the laughter in her eyes.

"Soft fur I can live with, but I absolutely forbid any hedgehogs in our bed. Is that understood?"

She looked down at the creature that now stood on its hind legs, its front claws pawing at the skirts of his coat. "You'll have to take it up with them," she said. Then, before he could argue the point, she grasped his hand; and surrounded by their four-legged companions, they started for the shelter of her cottage.

ABOUT THE AUTHOR

Janice Bennett lives with her family and a multitude of animals in Aromas, California. She is the author of over ten Zebra regency romances, including THE MATCHMAKING GHOST and A DESPERATE GAMBLE. Janice loves to hear from readers and you may write to her c/o Zebra Books. Please include a self-addressed stamped envelope if you wish a response.

CHARLOTTE'S KITTEN

Patricia Bray

Prologue

"George, you don't have to do this, you know," Thomas Dunne said. "After that bout of drinking last night, Archie Meredith can hardly sit his horse, and you aren't much better. Be a sensible man and give over. We can run the race another day."

From his perch on Sweet William's back, George Dawson looked down at his friend. "There's no need to make a fuss. It will be over in a trice, and then we can sit down to the fine breakfast your cook has prepared."

George smiled brightly to assure Thomas that all was well. But in truth his head hurt like the devil, and the morning sun nearly blinded him with its brilliance. Perhaps he had overindulged himself last night. But a wager was a wager, and Archie Meredith should never have made the mistake of disparaging the incomparable Sweet William.

The horse chose that moment to turn his head, opening his mouth to take a bite out of the unsuspecting Thomas Dunne.

George pulled the reins sharply. "None of your tricks now," he said.

Sweet William blew out his breath in a huff and began to paw the ground with one hoof. He and his master had done this before, and he knew that the group of excited men surrounding himself and the impertinent young gelding meant that soon he would have a chance to show the young horse and his lackluster master who was the real champion.

The horses and spectators milled impatiently just outside Riverdale's magnificent entryway. Gentlemen debated the merits of the two horses, placing wagers to show the sincerity of their opinions. Just beyond where the horses stood was the carriageway that led nearly a quarter mile to the gates, where the remainder of the spectators anxiously awaited the start of the race. The gravel drive was lined by ornamental hedges, while on either side spread out lush green lawns dotted with placidly grazing sheep.

The gentlemen present were all guests of Thomas Dunne. George Dawson had been there for over a week, taking advantage of his friend's hospitality. It had been a pleasant change after the frantic gaiety of the London Season, filled with fishing and shooting and all the gentlemanly pursuits. And Thomas could be counted on not to pester George about being the only old married man in their set of friends or to ask uncomfortable questions about why George had come to Riverdale rather than returning to his wife and his own estate.

Even Archie was a good sort, if none too competent a judge of horseflesh. George looked over at his opponent and was cheered to see that Archie looked as bad as he felt. Archie's face had a peculiar greenish cast, and he sat none too steady in the saddle.

Perhaps Thomas was right, and they should call it off. But before he could speak, the groom was clearing away the spectators and Archie maneuvered his horse alongside.

"Remember, first one to reach the gate wins," the groom instructed. He raised the pistol he was holding.

A pistol shot cracked the air.

Sweet William sprang forward, with Archie's mount close behind. George leaned forward, reveling in his horse's power. Sweet William was an unstoppable machine, seeming to increase speed with each stride.

"Come on, boy, show them what you're made of," George urged. The horse responded, and his lead grew until it was a length, and then two, and then more. He risked a quick glance back. Archie had fallen far behind. There was no chance that he could catch them. But still George urged his horse on to greater efforts, intent on proving Sweet William's prowess for once and for all.

A flicker of motion on his left caught his eye. And then a dog burst through the hedgerow and ran across the drive.

The sudden apparition startled Sweet William, who swerved and then stopped suddenly and reared back.

George reacted too late, his reflexes dulled by over-indulgence. At the last moment he shifted his weight and tightened his hold on the reins, frantically trying to stay in the saddle.

But it was no use. Time seemed to slow to a crawl as George was pitched backwards from the saddle. There was a brief blinding moment of pain as he landed on his back. And then he felt nothing. From a great distance he could hear shouts, but he could not make out the words. His head was tipped sideways, and all he could see was the bright white gravel of the drive.

A horse's legs came into view, and then a pair of boots beside them. Archie Meredith bent over him.

"Can you move? Are you injured?"

"I am fine," George said. He tried to push himself upright, but it was as if his limbs belonged to someone else. He could not move. With the beginnings of panic he realized he could not even feel his legs.

Thomas's face swam into view, wearing an unusual expression of concern.

"I don't think he can move," Archie whispered to Thomas. "And his leg is definitely broken."

It couldn't be broken. He would feel it if it were. He'd just had the wind knocked out of him, was all. George tried to speak, but words would not come. The summer morning which had seemed so bright just moments before began to grow dim. He was in real trouble now, and this time there was no getting out of it.

"Thomas," he whispered.

His friend knelt down beside him. He felt Thomas

clasp his hand, but soon that sensation, too, drifted away. The blackness grew closer and George realized that he was dying. He thought of his wife Charlotte. All he had ever wanted was to take care of her and see her happy. But now he was abandoning her for the last time.

"Charlotte," he whispered. He wished desperately that there were some way he could be sure that she would be taken care of. He struggled to speak, but the words would not come. *If only* . . . he thought. And then the darkness closed in, and he thought no more.

I

"Beg your pardon, Mrs. Dawson, but Ben Smith asks that you come to the stables, right quick."

Such summons had come all too frequent of late, so Charlotte Dawson did not look up from her writing desk. Her pen continued to flow smoothly across the paper. "Your letter was of much comfort to me, and I know Mr. Dawson would have been pleased at your remembrance," she wrote. Even now, three months after George's death, the letters of sympathy continued to arrive. Many of those who wrote were strangers to her, but with weeks of practice, she could now pen her acknowledgments almost by rote.

In a moment the letter was finished and she signed it. Only then did she look up. "What is it now?" she asked. "Has William bitten another stable boy? Did he break down the stall door?"

"I'm sure I don't know," the maid replied. "All I know is Ben Smith said you were to come quick."

Ben Smith met her at the entrance to the stables. A wiry, middle-aged man, he'd been George's personal groom in the old days. Now he and his helper Jeremiah were all who remained, as Charlotte had sold off most of George's horses and the staff had found positions elsewhere. Once bustling with activity and the score of hunters that George kept here, now the stable held but a pair of carriage horses and the gentle mare that George had given her for her birthday.

And Sweet William. She could never forget him.

Ben Smith led her into the stables. "Careful of your dress," he warned as they skirted the pile of straw and muck in the center of the aisle.

Charlotte surveyed the scene. All seemed quiet. The horses had been turned out to graze, and the stable boy Jeremiah was busy mucking out their stalls. They passed empty stall after empty stall, whose doors showed spots of lighter wood where once brass nameplates had gleamed. It was here in the stables that her husband had felt most comfortable, and it was here that she was reminded most of him. These days she avoided the stables as much as possible.

"What is it? I am in no mood for games," she said shortly.

Ben Smith only shook his head. He led her to the end of the stables where Sweet William stood in his loose box, placidly nosing through his hay. A small gray kitten lay curled between his feet, carefully grooming its paws, seemingly unaware of its danger.

"Where did it come from?"

"I dunno. It's not one of ours. But this morning, there it was."

It was a foolish kitten, indeed. Sweet William had always been high-strung, but since George's death he had turned downright vicious and unmanageable. Only the knowledge that George had loved the horse at least as much as he had loved her had kept Charlotte from ordering the animal destroyed.

"That is no place for a kitten, even if it is a stray," Charlotte declared. She unbolted the half door to the stall, preparing to rescue the small interloper. Till now Sweet William had attacked every one of his former handlers. She alone had been immune. She just hoped her luck would hold.

The thoroughbred lifted his head, but for once showed no signs of agitation. Charlotte stepped into the box slowly, trying not to spook the horse. "Easy now, I am just going to get your friend," she said.

Keeping her eye on Sweet William, she bent down and scooped up the kitten in one arm. Her prize secured, she began backing out of the box. The horse followed, not in a bolt as he was wont to do, but walking quietly, his eyes fixed on the kitten that she held in her arms.

Charlotte tried to swing the stall door shut, but it was blocked by the horse who stood half in and half out. "Now what?" she asked. The last time Sweet William had broken loose, it had taken a half-dozen men to recapture him.

She took another step backwards as Ben Smith began to edge between her and the horse. The kitten curled in her arms, enjoying his new perch. He began to purr. Sweet William's ears swiveled forward at the sound, and he stepped out of the box into the aisle. He advanced toward her, and then nuzzled the kitten gently.

The kitten accepted this tribute as his due. Charlotte held her breath, but nothing untoward happened. The unruly horse neither bolted nor lunged at his keepers. He might have been an entirely different animal.

"Witchcraft," she heard someone whisper.

"Nonsense," she replied automatically. She took another few steps to see what would happen. Sweet William ambled along after her.

Ben came over and grasped Sweet William by his halter. "I'm thinking if you had a mind to lead him, we might be able to turn him out in the small paddock," he said.

It was a ridiculous suggestion. Even if they managed to lead the horse to the paddock, how on earth would they ever convince him to return to his stall? The gray kitten looked up at her as if he, too, were urging her on.

Charlotte turned toward the door, and the gray kitten climbed out of her arms, his claws hooking in her wool shawl as he climbed to her shoulder. There he settled himself, a warm furry presence leaning against her neck. She began walking slowly out of the stables, and from behind her she could hear the clop of hooves as Sweet William followed along behind.

They reached the paddock without incident, and Sweet William was turned loose within for the first time in weeks. The kitten leaped down from her shoulder onto the top rail of the fence. With tail held high he stalked his way along the rail, then jumped up to the top of a post, where he curled up to bask in the warm sunshine.

Sweet William looked over at the kitten, and apparently convinced that all was well, he began to graze. Charlotte laughed to see the great horse apparently fascinated by this smallest of kittens.

"See that the kitten gets a saucer of cream," she ordered.

It was a crisp and sunny autumn day, a welcome relief after several days of steady rain. Standing at the windows of the breakfast room, Sir Robert Harrington looked out on a clear blue sky and the waterlogged grounds of his host's estate. Even without the pouring rain to fight against, the soaked ground would make harvesting difficult, and he wondered how the workers on his own estate were faring.

"See? I told you last night that the rain would stop today," Lord Grimbley said as he entered the room. His white hair stuck out in a fringe around his balding head, and from the mud still clinging to his boots it was clear that he had already been outside this morning.

"I had faith that it would," Sir Robert replied, turning to face his host.

Lord Grimbley poured a cup of tea for himself and took two slices of toast in his hand. He did not sit, but rather stood next to the table eating, as if every moment were precious. "I've already been out to the fields, and they are a mire. It will be at least a day before we can start bringing in the grain and use the new thresher."

"I thought as much." Sir Robert took the news calmly. He had come two hundred miles to see the new thresher and to see for himself the other innovations that Lord Grimbley had made at Stony Hill. Another few days were of no consequence.

"Cartwright and myself will be going over to the home farm," Lord Grimbley said, referring to his able steward. "A stream there came over the banks and damaged several of the tenants' cottages. We can hardly spare a man till after the harvest is in, but I want to take a look for myself and see what needs to be done."

Robert took the hint. "I am certain I can occupy myself," he said, although it would be difficult to pass the time. It was not that the household was empty, but rather that it was too full, filled with the friends of Lord Grimbley's eldest son Stephen, come for the shooting and the annual hunt ball. They were a wild and rackety set, and Robert had no wish to become closer acquainted with them.

Lord Grimbley swallowed the last of his tea with a gulp and then crammed several slices of toast into the pockets of his coat. As he prepared to leave, a thought seemed to occur to him. "You could always tag along with Geoffrey Osborne. He said last night that he would be riding over to Torringford. The widow is selling off the last of George Dawson's hunters. He had a great reputation for breeding horses, if you care for that sort of thing."

Robert made a noncommittal noise, and his host left the room. Only then did he sink down into a chair, deep in thought.

So, Charlotte was still here. He had known she lived in the county, but not till he had arrived had he realized how close Torringford lay to Stony Hill.

Strange to think of Charlotte as a widow. It seemed only yesterday that she had been a mischievous child, begging him and George to allow her to tag along. Two years younger than himself and George, she had been a wild hoyden, intent on proving that she could race and fish and hunt as well as any boy. He had bandaged up her scrapes, shared childish confidences, and been honored to receive her first awkward kiss.

And then overnight she had left his life, gone to become George's wife. For eight years they had not seen each other. Had not spoken. And now she was a widow.

George Dawson's death had come as a great shock. Though they had not spoken for years, it was not until there was no possibility of reconciliation that Robert realized how much he had missed his friend. And how he had always cherished the unspoken belief that someday they would once again be friends. But he had been too stubborn to make the first move, and now the opportunity was gone forever.

He had sent a letter of condolences to Charlotte and received a polite, if formal, reply. But he would not call on her. She would not want to see him. Not after the way that they had parted. And he did not know if he wanted to see her. There was no sense in stirring up old wounds. Best to let the past lie in peace.

She would not be there, he told himself as he and Geoffrey Osborne rode through the streets of Torringford. It was unlikely that she would be home. Or even if she were, a woman would have no reason to be in the stables. A groom or a steward would show the horse and handle the transaction. He had only accompanied Osborne out of boredom.

They stopped in the village for directions and discovered that Mrs. Dawson resided on a small estate just outside the town. Her residence turned out to be a neat, gray-stone manor house. Modest compared to the great hall she had been raised in, it was, nonetheless, the grandest house in the neighborhood.

Surveying the property with an experienced gaze, he saw that the lane was well-maintained, the fences in good repair, and the fields he passed had already been harvested. A few workers could be seen preparing the fields for winter. It was a tranquil scene.

Mr. Osborne turned his horse in the direction of the stables, and Robert followed. The stables were even finer than the house, probably built during George Dawson's tenure. Here, too, all spoke of order and prosperity. It should have comforted him to see Charlotte living so well; yet, instead, he felt oddly disappointed.

A boy came out of the stables and held their horses as they dismounted.

"We're here to take a look at Sweet William. I

understand he is still for sale," Geoffrey Osborne said.

The boy grinned. "Oh, yes. Indeed, he is. Ain't no one gonna take on a horse as mean as that. Why last time a swell came here, Willy took one look and—"

"That will be enough, Jeremiah."

It was her voice. He had never forgotten the sound of it. He turned, and he could see a figure standing in the door to the stables, silhouetted against the darkness inside. And then Charlotte stepped out into the sunlight.

His breath caught in his throat. Gone was the girl he remembered, all awkward angles and budding curves that only hinted at the future. Now the dark-gray riding habit she wore clung to curves that would tempt a saint. Even her face had changed, her freckles faded and her once-orange hair turned to gorgeous auburn.

Osborne stood closest to the stable, so it was to him that she turned first. "I was expecting a Mr. Osborne," she said.

"Geoffrey Osborne, at your service," he replied. Osborne's eyes widened as he took stock of the beautiful widow. "And may I say if I had known what beauty lay here, I would have made the journey without delay, despite the torrential rains."

What a fatuous speech. His opinion of Geoffrey Osborne fell a notch. Robert gave a small cough.

"May I present Sir Robert Harrington, who accompanied me today."

Robert stepped out from behind his horse. "Mrs. Dawson. Please accept my sympathy for your recent loss. I know you must miss your husband greatly."

Charlotte's eyes widened when she saw him, but her composure remained unmarred. "I thank you for your kind sentiments," she said, and Osborne belatedly rushed to offer his sympathies as well.

He felt awkward, unsure of his welcome. Charlotte had changed in more than appearance. The old Charlotte would never have greeted him in such a way. She would have berated him soundly for the impertinence of calling or run and hugged him if she were pleased to see him. With the old Charlotte one never had to wonder what she was feeling. But the widowed Mrs. Dawson was an entirely different creature.

Robert! What was he doing here? Her heart stopped for a moment when he came into view. She had thought of him often in these last months, but never had she imagined that he would come to her. Robert had always been a serious boy, but from his appearance he'd become even more serious and reserved as a man. She found herself staring at him, but she could not help it. What did you say to a stranger who had once been closer to you than a brother?

"Mrow," She felt something brush against her skirt and, looking down, saw that the elusive kitten had deigned to make an appearance.

"Where have you been?" she asked. The servants had taken to calling the kitten Ghost after its gray coloring and habit of appearing and disappearing seemingly into thin air. "William has missed you."

The kitten circled her skirts till he stood slightly in front of her, regarding the two gentleman with an unblinking stare.

"If you would care to show us the horse, Mrs. Dawson—" Mr. Osborne prompted. He did not appear pleased at being ignored in favor of a kitten. A smallish man in build, he did not have the look of a sportsman. Nor could she see any signs of the strength of character it would take to command the temperamental steed. But he had come all this way and it would not be fair to turn him away now.

"Of course . . . if you will follow me." She bent down and scooped up Ghost, who eagerly climbed to his preferred perch on her shoulder.

Robert hung back, so she found herself speaking with Mr. Osborne. "As you can see, we have already sold off the other hunters. Only Sweet William remains. He was my late husband's favorite, but even George found him a challenge at times."

"I like a challenge," Mr. Osborne said. But he was looking at her, and not at the horse.

They reached the loose box, and Sweet William whickered happily upon seeing his friend. Ghost jumped off her shoulder onto the half door and then sat on the railing in the manner of a king surveying his domain.

The two men admired the horse and commented to each other about his conformation and breeding. Intent on examining his teeth, Mr. Osborne tried to grab his halter, but Sweet William would have none of it, backing away and stamping his feet.

"What say you have him saddled and I give him a try?" Mr. Osborne suggested.

"Of course," she said, signaling to Ben Smith, who had stood quietly waiting with Sweet William's tack. She would not wager a farthing on Mr. Osborne's chances of remaining in the saddle for a quarter hour. But she disliked the way he kept looking at her and saw no reason to warn him.

Ben led the horse into the aisle and began tacking him up. Sweet William stood quietly for the operation. He'd lost some of his wildness since the arrival of the kitten, but he could still be difficult to manage when he chose. Out he stepped of his stall, his great size was easy to appreciate. Sixteen hands high at his withers, he dwarfed Mr. Osborne, who could barely see over the horse's saddle.

She led the gentlemen out into the courtyard, and the groom followed with Sweet William. Ben adjusted the stirrups and held the reins so Mr. Osborne could mount.

Mr. Osborne approached the horse, put one hand on the saddle, and then stepped back again. "He's a big brute, isn't he?" Mr. Osborne said. He no longer looked eager for a chance to prove his skill.

Charlotte took pity on him. "Indeed, he is not to everyone's taste."

Mr. Osborne looked at Sweet William, then back at her. "No, I can see he won't suit at all. Over-large horses tire easily, and I need a hunter who can keep up with the field."

Only a fool would disparage Sweet William, who

had carried George through many a long day of sport
with never a sign of fatigue. But Charlotte held her
tongue.

"It takes a fine gentleman to understand horses as
you do," Ben Smith said. Luckily Mr. Osborne did
not seem to notice the sarcasm.

"You've got long legs there yourself, Sir Robert.
Why don't you take him through his paces?" Mr.
Osborne suggested.

Robert shook his head in refusal. "No, I don't think
so."

She fixed him with a sharp gaze. "Why not? You
came here to see the horse, didn't you?"

"Indeed," he said. Collecting the reins from Ben,
he mounted with ease. Sweet William tossed his head
and danced a little, but Robert swiftly brought him
under control.

"There's a good path off to the left. Takes you
through a field, then round the ornamental pond,"
Ben offered.

Robert rode off in the direction Ben had indicated.
She did not stay to wait for his return. She could not.
He looked so right up there. What would she say if
he decided he wanted the horse? And how would
George have felt about her giving his most beloved
possession to his former best friend?

She retreated back into the stable, needing a
moment to gather her composure. Robert's appearance had stirred up feelings she'd thought long since
gone. You are no longer a child, she told herself.
You are a grown woman. A widow. And Robert is an
acquaintance. Nothing more.

There was a footstep behind her. She spun around and saw that Mr. Osborne had followed her inside.

"Is there something I can help you with?" she asked.

Mr. Osborne came towards her. She did not like the expression on his face and took a few steps backwards. "I see your husband had an eye for more than just fine horses."

Charlotte glanced around, but save for the horses they were alone. Ben was outside, awaiting Robert's return, and the stable boy was no doubt busy elsewhere.

"A beautiful woman such as yourself must find this time so very . . . lonely," Mr. Osborne insinuated. "I could tell at once you were a woman of passion. You need a gentleman who can understand you."

How dare this wretch proposition her? "Your words do you no credit," she said. "If you are the gentleman you claim to be, then you will remove yourself at once."

But he did not leave. He advanced toward her, and she retreated until her back was up against the stable wall. She was not afraid, but rather annoyed. Mr. Osborne was not the first so-called gentleman to offer to comfort a new-made widow. But in the past she had been able to discourage the cads with a few well-chosen words.

"You must leave at once or I will call for help," she said.

He licked his lips in a repulsive gesture. "Call away, but I know this is what you are longing for," he said, leaning forward to kiss her.

She raised her right hand and slapped his face as hard as she could. "How dare you insult me!"

Mr. Osborne's expression turned ugly, and for the first time she began to feel afraid.

"No need to be coy," Mr. Osborne said. He reached for her, and she opened her mouth to call for help.

From the corner of her eye she saw a blur of movement as Ghost launched himself at the intruder. He dove at Mr. Osborne's face, screeching, claws extended. The furry missile was too much for Mr. Osborne, who stumbled backwards and landed in the pile of muck and straw.

"My eyes!" he screamed, holding his hands across his brow.

She felt a grim satisfaction. It would serve him right if the kitten had blinded him. Anyone who would take advantage of a defenseless widow deserved no less.

She would have treated him to the tongue-lashing he deserved, but then Ben and Jeremiah came running in, summoned by Osborne's screeching.

"Take your hands off your face so we can see what's wrong," she said impatiently.

Mr. Osborne lowered his hands, and she could see that he had suffered naught but scratches on one cheek. He blinked a few times, as if to test his vision.

"Well, no harm done, not that you didn't deserve more," she said. "I suggest you remove yourself at once."

Mr. Osborne struggled to sit up, cursing as he put one hand into a clod of manure. No one moved to help him, and eventually he managed to struggle to his feet.

"But these pantaloons are ruined! And my gloves as well. You can not mean this."

He made such a pathetic sight that she bit her tongue to keep from laughing. "You should have thought of that before," she said.

Ben shook his pitchfork in the direction of the hapless Mr. Osborne. "I'd be happy to clean up this mess for you," he offered.

"I think Mr. Osborne has learned his lesson," she said. She knew her servants were fiercely loyal, and she was afraid Ben might try and teach Mr. Osborne a lesson of his own. While it was one thing to defend his mistress if she were under attack, having Ben harm Mr. Osborne now would only cause trouble. "Just see that he departs at once."

Ben nodded, and she knew she could trust him to do what she asked and no more.

"Mr. Osborne, if you ever set foot on my property again, I will set the dogs on you. Do you understand?"

"Yes," he muttered.

"Good," she said. "And, Ben, please ask Sir Robert Harrington to come inside when he returns."

As she left the stableyard, she noticed the kitten was following alongside. Charlotte reached down and scooped him up. "Brave little warrior," she said, holding him close and stroking his head. "You are more of a gentleman now than that Osborne will ever be."

The kitten gave her a look as if to say, "What else

did you expect?'' And then he yawned, spoiling the impression of fierceness. Charlotte laughed and settled the kitten in her arms.

"Come with me and we'll see if Cook can find you a fitting reward.''

II

Robert rode away slowly. He resisted the urge to look back to see if she were watching him. He concentrated instead on getting the feel for the horse. Sweet William started along quietly enough, eagerly breaking into a canter when they reached the open field. But when Robert signaled for a trot, the horse ignored him as if his rider were inconsequential. A less experienced rider might have jerked at the reins or cursed the beast, but instead Robert merely tightened the reins slowly, pulling the horse's head in until he had no choice but to comply.

Sweet William swung into a trot as if it had been his own idea all along; and when Robert asked him to walk, he did so with only the slightest of hesitations. As they passed through the small woods he made a start towards the trees, intent on brushing his rider off. But Robert had anticipated this trick and kept the horse on the path.

"You're a clever devil, aren't you? I can see why George was so fond of you."

As children, George had loved a challenge. He had been the wild one, always looking to prove himself. With only three-months difference in their ages, the two boys had shared their childhood pastimes. But it had been George who'd been the first to graduate to a real horse after he'd borrowed his father's hunter, and George who'd nearly drowned when teaching himself how to swim. George had been the first to break his arm, and later the first to be sent down from school.

And then Charlotte, two years younger, began escaping her schoolroom, begging to be included in their adventures. At first George had refused her pleas. After all, Charlotte was a mere baby, all of seven years of age, compared to the boys who were very nearly ten. But when she proved as game as any lad to join their games, not to mention being the proud possessor of a pony who had been taught tricks, the boys had grudgingly allowed Charlotte to join in.

Georgie, Robbie, and Charlie. They'd been inseparable, best of friends. Three young hellions, according to their families and the villagers. They'd sworn that nothing could ever break their friendship. But even friendship had its limits, as they'd discovered that autumn day eight years ago. On that day the bond had been broken, and Robert had lost part of his soul.

But he did not want to think of that day, or of

the part he had played in ending their friendship. Instead, he gave the horse his head. "Come on, show me what you're made of," he said.

When he returned to the stableyard, Sweet William had broken into a light sweat. But his breathing was steady and Robert knew the horse could have run for hours.

The middle-aged groom came out to meet him. "He went well for you?"

Robert swung out of the saddle and handed the reins to the groom. "Yes, indeed. I'd swear he was disappointed when we turned back here."

The groom nodded. "This one would run all day if you gave him his head. It's why Master George loved him so much for the hunting."

Robert looked around, but saw no sign of Geoffrey Osborne. "Is Mr. Osborne inside?"

The groom's mouth tightened as if he had bitten into something sour. "Indeed not. Your friend made himself unwelcome, so Mrs. Dawson asked him to leave."

"He's not my friend. Just an acquaintance," Robert felt compelled to explain.

The groom still eyed him askance.

"I trust Mr. Osborne did not insult her? Mrs. Dawson is a good friend of mine. As was her husband. I know George would have wanted me to protect Charlotte, should there have been a need." If that rake Osborne had harmed Charlotte, Robert would wring his neck. And enjoy doing it.

"Nothing serious. Mrs. Dawson put him in his place right smartly. And it will be quite awhile before he thinks to try the like again." The groom smiled in remembrance of Osborne's comeuppance. "She asked that you come in the house and speak with her before you leave."

A maid showed him to what looked like the house-keeper's room. Charlotte sat at a small desk, a book of accounts open before her. There were inkstains on her fingers, and her brow was furrowed in thought.

"Still having trouble with your sums?"

"Not that I'd ever take help from you. You were worse at math than I was," she said, looking up at him.

"Really? I seem to recall you never did master your eleven times-tables."

"And I have yet to need them, so that proves I was right all along," she said.

"Touché."

She grinned, and for the first time he could see the echo of the mischievous girl who had once been his friend. He felt a strange sensation, as if some long frozen part of him were finally coming back to life. He smiled back at her, but something in his expression must have discomfited her, for her grin faded and her eyes looked away.

She looked down at her desk, seeming absorbed in straightening the papers and laying the pen back in the inkstand.

"I can finish this anytime," she said, rising from her seat. "Come to the parlor, and let me offer you some refreshment. We have fresh cider, or perhaps you would prefer something stronger?"

He chose cider and followed her into a formal

sitting room. She sat down on a velvet sofa, and he picked a chair opposite.

The silence stretched awkwardly between them. He wondered why she had asked to see him.

"What did you think of Sweet William?" she finally asked.

"A fine horse," he said noncommittally.

"He didn't give you any trouble? No, of course not," she said, answering her own question before he could speak. "You were always a good rider. Better than George, though he would never admit it."

The name George hung in the air between them, reminding him of all that had gone before. "About what happened that October . . ."

"Don't," she said, raising a hand to cut off his words. "There is no need to explain. It was kind of you to call today. I have thought of you often in these months, since . . . since George's passing."

She looked so forlorn that he wanted to take her in his arms and comfort her. But he remained in his seat, his impulse checked by the knowledge that such an embrace was not proper. And by the knowledge that he did not know how Charlotte would react. He had lost the right to comfort her years ago, when he had lost her friendship. Now the only support he could offer was the knowledge that he shared her grief.

"I was truly sorry when I heard the news," he said. It sounded trite, but he was not good at expressing his emotions. How could he tell her that the news had shaken him to the core, making him question everything about his own existence? George may have died, but he and Charlotte had had eight years together as husband and wife. They had moved forward, while Robert had been frozen in the past. He had little to show for the last eight years, save a catalogue of improvements to his land and a reputation for respectable dullness.

"I know George regretted the loss of your friendship as much as I did. It seems stupid now that we quarreled over such a thing."

It had not seemed a small matter at the time. It had seemed like betrayal. Deeply hurt and angry, Robert had uttered accusations that he had lived to regret.

"I should have apologized long ago," he said finally.

"Yes. But the blame is ours as well. We never gave you an opportunity to do so."

It was true. He'd seen Charlotte only thrice during these years, and always at a distance. She'd never returned to her home, nor had she accompanied George when he visited his family. Seldom had she ventured to London, although George had been a fixture there each Season. In the past he'd considered her absence a blessing, but now he wondered if they might not have made up the quarrel sooner had the three of them been thrown together in company.

"I would like it very much if we could be friends again," she said. "Somehow I think George would have liked that as well."

George was gone forever. It was too late to make amends to him, but by reclaiming his friendship with Charlotte, perhaps he could reclaim a portion of his past. "I can think of nothing I would like better," Robert admitted. "If there is ever anything I can do for you—"

"Actually there is," she said. "Would you consider taking Sweet William off my hands?"

The horse? "I don't really have need for a hunter—"

"I know. But you saw what a handful he can be. Sweet William is growing stale and ill-tempered without exercise. I've tried to find a buyer, but the only men who've offered for him were brutal riders. George cared for that horse more than any other creature. I can't give the horse to someone who will ill-treat him," she said firmly.

"But what about his friends?" Surely one of them would want the horse. Mourning George was bad enough, without taking on such a visible reminder of his late friend.

Charlotte shrugged. "George had many friends, but I am not acquainted with most of them. I'd never met Mr. Dunne until he came to me with the news that George had been killed in an accident on his estate. I hadn't even known George had gone to the country. I'd thought him still fixed in London."

Her words troubled him. A wife should have known her husband's friends. Not to mention his whereabouts.

"I'd be happy to take the horse on, until I can find a suitable buyer." It was the least he could do for her.

"Thank you," she said.

The servants arrived with a light luncheon. While

he ate, they reminisced about their childhood. They took turns sharing memories of George and of the adventures they'd had. He noticed that they were each careful to avoid any mention of that last summer.

Charlotte asked about his mother, and he shared news of home. She seemed genuinely interested, so he described some of the improvements he had made to his estate and his plans for a acquiring a new threshing machine like the one Lord Grimbley had demonstrated.

In turn she recounted a little of her life at the manor. But there were gaps in her account that told a tale of their own. It was not what she said, but what she did not say that bothered him. There was no mention of George's presence, except when she referred to his horses.

Despite her marriage, it sounded more and more as if she and George had lived very separate lives. It was a thought which disturbed him. Over the years he had reconciled himself to George and Charlotte's marriage, believing that it was a love match. He'd hoped they had found happiness together. But though no words of criticism escaped her lips, it was clear that whatever passion George and Charlotte had once shared had grown cold.

He spent the afternoon with Charlotte, staying far longer than propriety dictated. Finally he could postpone his departure no longer. As it was, he would be lucky to make it back to Stony Hill before nightfall.

They agreed that he would return in a week's time to fetch Sweet William. Charlotte escorted him outside and waited with him as a groom brought his horse.

As he prepared to mount, he turned back to Charlotte and voiced the question that had troubled him all afternoon. "I know I have no right to ask, but pray tell me, were you happy?"

There was a moment of silence. "I was content," she said.

He nodded, choking down a sudden surge of anger. Charlotte deserved more than mere contentment.

She knew from the flash of anger in his eyes that it had been the wrong thing to say. But she could not lie to him. Robert had always known her too well. He would have seen through her lies in a moment.

Words trembled on the tip of her tongue, but Charlotte bit them back. She owed Robert no explanations. Let him draw his own conclusions. Marriages were not the stuff of a young girl's dreams. Most marriages were alliances between families, arranged for financial or social reasons. She and George had been no more or less happy than most couples.

A marriage based on friendship was more than many had. It had taken time to adjust to their new roles, but after a while she and George had achieved a comfortable routine. What matter if George's absences from home had grown longer and longer, till she would go months without seeing him? Each spring he would swoop down and fetch her to London to celebrate her birthday. And he always returned to Torringford for the hunting season and the harvest.

It was not as if she'd lacked occupation. Tilden Hall had been a gift from George's parents upon their wedding. Unoccupied for several years, the estate had been in dreadful condition when the newlyweds arrived. George had taken one look at the place and promptly decamped for London.

But Charlotte had been intrigued by the possibilities and stayed, throwing herself into the task of restoring the hall to its former glory. Once that was accomplished, she began involving herself in the running of the home farm, and then later in starting a school for the children of the tenants.

She'd kept herself so busy that there was no time to notice if there were anything lacking in her life. As a child she'd defined herself by her rebellion against her parents' strict ways. Now she developed a new sense of self-worth. She learned patience and responsibility and worked hard to earn the respect of her neighbors and tenants.

Though Charlotte felt she'd matured, George was still the same as he'd always been. Always cheerful, always ready for a lark or to hare off on a mad adventure with his friends. Each time he came home, they found they had less and less in common with each other.

Maybe if they had had children, things would have been different. But it was not to be. And each year the marriage grew harder for her to endure.

Then George had been killed in that stupid race. Though her grief had been more for the boy he had been than the husband he had become, she had still mourned him sincerely.

As the weeks passed, the worst of her grief subsided and she began to realize that George's death had set her free. She felt guilty for thinking of freedom when the cost had been her husband's life. She reminded herself that she had been a dutiful wife; and if George were still alive, she would have honored her vows and stayed with him forever.

But he was gone, and now for the first time in her adult life she had possibilities. No longer did the future stretch out before her in unimaginable bleakness. She could stay here in Torringford. She could go to London or to see her sister Cecilia in Bath or to anywhere else her fancy took her. The possibilities were at once exhilarating and frightening.

The one thing she would not do was return home to her parents. After not seeing her for eight years, they'd had the impertinence to attend George's funeral and then begin giving orders as if she were still their sixteen-year-old daughter. Charlotte was to return home with them at once, they'd declared. It was not fit that she live at Tilden Hall alone. Never mind that she'd lived here on her own for much of her marriage. Now that she was widowed, her parents felt a perfect right to begin dictating her life. As soon as her year of mourning was over, no doubt they would try to marry her off to a widower or some other gentleman who met their rigid standards of propriety.

She'd declined their offer, politely but firmly. She had no intention of letting them force her into another marriage. She had spent the last eight years paying for her youthful folly. Surely she had earned the right to a measure of happiness.

No longer given to impulsive decisions, Charlotte had thought carefully about what form her future would take. She would stay here in Torringford, of course, until her full year of mourning was over. And then she would start to take her place in society. She would not seek a husband, but it would be good to expand her circle of acquaintances.

But now there was Robert, throwing all her careful considerations into disarray. She had thought about him often, but never really expected that he would want to see her again. Then he had come, looking as kind and reliable as he had always been. Her mind told her that he had come as a friend. But her heart, still ruled by the headstrong girl she had once been, began to nourish impossible hopes.

III

Robert was coming to see her. Today. In the seven days since his visit she had relived every moment of their time together. She had spent hours thinking of him, wondering if their meeting had been mere happenstance or if he had purposely sought her out. Was it possible that he still cared for her? Dared she hope that his feelings ran deeper than mere friendship?

For herself, she did not know how to feel toward him. As a young girl she had fancied herself in love with Robert. But the fates had intervened; and with her marriage to George, she'd found the only way not to hurt was to put all thoughts of Robert aside. It had helped that she never expected to see him again. How could she have known that the mere sight

of him would be enough to bring back the dreams
she'd thought forgotten long ago?

Charlotte Dawson, you are a scandalous woman, she
scolded herself. Widowed a mere four months, and
already dreaming of another man. What would her
parents say? What would George think, if he could
see her now?

And how would Robert react if he knew how much
he had occupied her thoughts this last week?

Charlotte jumped up from her seat by the window,
where she had spent the last hour watching the lane
that led to the manor. She could not sit still any
longer. Wrapping herself in a cloak against the chill
October day, she went out to the barn to ensure that
all was in readiness for Robert's arrival.

She found Sweet William in his stall, placidly chew-
ing on his hay. As she approached, the horse lifted
his head and poked it out the stall door.

"You were a rare handful," she said, gently stroking
his nose. "But we will miss you all the same."

It struck her that she would likely not see the horse
again. She felt suddenly sad, as if she were cutting
the last tie that bound her to her late husband. True
she still had Tilden Hall, but the estate had always
been more her domain than his. George had come
to seem like a guest here during his infrequent visits.

Sweet William gave her what she fancied was a
reproachful look. "Don't worry," she said. "Robert
is a kind man. He will see that you are well taken
care of."

"Mrow." The kitten rubbed against her ankles.

"Good morning, Ghost. Where did you come

from?'' she asked. She'd looked for the kitten earlier, but hadn't seen a trace of him.

He stood before her crying plaintively till she bent down and picked him up. Holding him in one arm, she began scratching around his ears until he purred in contentment.

"Did you want to see me, Mrs. Dawson?'' Ben Smith asked, coming up beside her.

"No, I just came to see that all was in readiness.''

"I saw to things myself. Sweet William has been fed and watered, and the blacksmith was by yesterday to fix that loose left front shoe. He will be in fine trim for his new master.''

Fortunately Ben Smith did not question her sudden interest in the running of the stable. Nor did he mention that this was her second visit this morning.

Charlotte nodded, but still she lingered.

"Sweet William will be in good hands,'' Ben offered, as if he sensed her misgivings.

"Of course,'' she said, and then she forced herself to leave. If she stayed any longer, Ben would think her gone strange. She set the kitten down, and the kitten promptly leaped to the top of the half door and then down into the straw that lined Sweet William's stall. The horse nuzzled his friend briefly before returning to his hay.

Seeing the two animals together, she realized that it might be impossible to separate them. *I hope Robert still likes kittens,* she thought.

Leaving the stables, she began walking toward the formal gardens, hoping the stroll would calm her thoughts. As she passed by the entrance to the fields, she encountered Jeremiah, the young stable boy. His arms were filled with a half-dozen freshly dug mangle-wurzels, and he ducked his head nervously when he saw her.

She bit back a smile. In Torringford, it was the custom on All Hallow's Eve for young men to carve lanterns out of mangle-wurzels and to carry them through the countryside as they carried out pranks. But it was all in fun, and no real harm was ever done.

"Just don't let Ben catch you with those," she cautioned. "He doesn't hold with such things."

"Thank you, ma'am," Jeremiah said. Clearly he had expected her to scold him.

"And if I am not mistaken, Mrs. Stickney has been saving candle ends for you," Charlotte said, referring to her formidable cook. "If you knock at the kitchen door, I am certain she will let you have them."

"Yes, ma'am. Thank you, ma'am."

She went on her way, smiling at the foolishness of youth. But her thoughts turned dark as she remembered her own folly at that age. At least Jeremiah's pranks were unlikely to ruin any lives.

She wondered if Robert ever thought about that night. It seemed a strange twist of fate that they would once more be brought together, with tonight All Hallow's Eve.

She remembered all too well her last days as a heedless child. Robert and George had finished school the previous spring. Naively she had imagined that they would spend the summers together as they had always done. But her friends were young men now, and less inclined to spend time with a girl who was still in the schoolroom. Instead, they spent much of that summer in London with their parents, and then in house parties with friends they had made at school.

Then autumn came, and Robert and George had returned for the hunting season. No longer her constant companions, they were, nonetheless, her friends and visited her nearly as often as they had before. Bored with the preparations for her elder sister's wedding, Charlotte had rejoiced in their presence.

And then it was All Hallow's Eve, and Charlotte had begged them to take her to see the village bonfire as they had done when they were children. Robert had refused, saying that she was too old for such a childish prank. But after he left, Charlotte had managed to convince George to be her companion. Little had she known that that night she would ruin not one life but three.

It was early afternoon when Robert arrived at Tilden Hall in his traveling coach. He planned to ride Sweet William for the rest of the journey. He preferred being on horseback to riding in the closed carriage, particularly when the weather was fine. The exercise would do Sweet William good and ensure the horse was too tired to cause any mischief once they reached the inn that was their destination that night.

A footman opened the carriage door for him, and he descended into the courtyard.

"Pull the carriage around back, and then why don't

you see if the kitchen will offer you a glass of ale? I must speak with Mrs. Dawson, so it will be a short while before we go on," Robert instructed his coachman.

The coachman nodded, touching the brim of his hat.

He looked up to see Charlotte coming down the stairs to greet him.

"Mrs. Dawson," he said, conscious of the watching servants.

"Sir Robert," she replied equally formally, her welcoming smile fading.

"If I might have a few moments of your time?"

He did not wait for a reply, but linked her arm in his. They strolled around the corner and into the formal gardens that graced the south side of the house. At this time of the year there was little to see, save the fading glories of the marigolds and chrysanthemums. Fallen beech leaves dotted the walkways, waiting to be swept up.

He looked at Charlotte. She was as he remembered from last week. Still glorious, but the sober widow's blacks did not suit her. She should dress in colors. Warm ambers and reds would suit her far better than dull black.

"What is so important that you must drag me out here?" she asked.

"I still owe you an apology—"

"Enough," she said. She tried to pull her arm free from his, but he held on to her. "I do not wish to discuss it."

"But I do," he insisted. "I said terrible things to you. And to George." He had accused George of deliberately seducing her and Charlotte of being no better than a lightskirt. "There can be no excuse."

He could still remember how shattered he had felt when the gossip came that young Charlotte Dawson had been caught in a compromising position. And to discover that it had been his best friend George who had been accused of seducing her. He had known that it could not be true, but then the news had come that George and Charlotte were to marry. It had felt like betrayal. It had felt like the end of the world.

"You were wrong to act as you did," she said. "We needed your friendship then more than ever. But you believed the worst that gossip had to say and cast us aside."

Her words hurt, but she said nothing that he did not already know. "I was a poor friend," he said. "I was angry with you and George. I also felt guilty, for if I had come with you that night, it might never have happened."

She stopped and turned to face him. "You? Guilty? If there is any blame, it is mine."

He stared at her. The words were on the tip of his tongue, but he would not ask her what had really happened that night.

"I was still a willful child back then," she said. "After you left that afternoon, I convinced George to come with me to the village. The bonfire was glorious that year."

She smiled sadly in remembrance. "I knew some of the village girls, and they invited me to join them in casting nuts and telling fortunes. George soon wandered off and began drinking. It was all great fun until it was midnight and time to leave."

She paused.

"You don't have to tell me this," he said. But he hoped that she would.

"I do," she insisted. "When I went to find George, he was lying at the smithy's, so drunk he could barely stand. I did not want to leave him there, so I put his arm around my shoulders and began walking home. He held on to me for dear life, and when he tripped, he tore my dress. Finally I managed to get him as far as his own estate. I left him there, and returned home. It was just my bad luck that Lady Morehead could not sleep that night and that she saw me as I crept back to my room."

He released his breath slowly. "And she felt obliged to inform your parents?"

Charlotte shook her head. "Worse yet. She let out a screech that woke the house. There I was, with my dress torn and muddy and my hair hanging down around my waist. You can imagine what everyone thought."

Indeed, he could. It was what he had thought himself. The evidence against her had seemed overwhelming.

"Did you not try to explain?"

"My parents believed the worst of me," she said bitterly. "They always had. They demanded to know whom I had been with, but I refused to tell. They locked me in my room and threatened never to let me out. But I knew I was innocent. I could have borne any punishment."

"So, when did they realize it was George?"

"They suspected you and George right off, but your parents could vouch for your whereabouts and those who were in the village said that George had paid me no heed and left early. No one knew that he had been there the whole time, passed out in the smithy."

She kicked at some leaves with her boot, venting her anger on them. "Lord Morehead threatened to call off the marriage between his son and Cecilia. He said that he would never allow his heir to marry into a family with such a dubious reputation. I still don't know if I would have confessed, but before I could decide, George called on my father and offered to make amends. My parents couldn't wait to wash their hands of me. We were married as soon as a special license could be found."

At the time the hasty marriage had seemed the confirmation of his worst fears. But he knew he should have had more faith in her, and in George. He tasted bitter regret that he had allowed his jealousy to get the better of him.

"I am sorry," he said. "I did not know."

"How could you? They would not let me see you, except for the day of the wedding. George and I were angry because we had hoped for your support, but you seemed determined to think the worst of us. Only later did I realize how it must have looked to you."

He turned his head so he could see her expression, wanting to gauge her reaction to his next words. "I was angry that day. Angry because I had thought we might make a match of it. And then it seemed as if George had once again beaten me to the prize."

She looked at him in astonishment. "Why did you not say something?"

Because he had been a coward. "I was young, and you were still in the schoolroom. It seemed wrong to speak of my feelings. Later I was glad I had said nothing, for it seemed you and George were suited for each other."

He had thought her in love with George. Enough in love that she had cast convention and modesty to the winds. And he had hated her for it.

She looked at him searchingly. "I am sorry you were hurt," she said. "I did not know."

He had barely known himself. Not till he had lost Charlotte had he realized how much he cared for her.

"Can you find it in your heart to forgive me for my hasty words?" he asked.

"I forgave you long ago," she said. "Perhaps things turned out for the best after all. The girl I was then would have made you a very poor wife."

Ah, but he had loved her then. And he suspected that he was falling in love with the woman she had become. Should he tell her of his feelings? Or should he wait, rather than jeopardize their renewed friendship? A true gentleman would not think of courting her until a full year had passed. But dare he wait that long again?

A young stable boy came running round the corner of the house. He stopped as he caught up to them. "My lord, Ben Smith said to find you and tell you that your horses are growing restless. Should we unhitch them from the carriage? Or will you be journeying on?"

Robert looked at Charlotte, but she did not urge him to stay. "Tell him I will be leaving presently," he said.

"Yes, my lord," the stable boy said, running back in the direction of the stables.

He and Charlotte followed more sedately. "Have your parents invited you to visit for Christmas?"

She grimaced. "Yes, but the invitation was buried in a letter scolding me for shaming the family by choosing to stay here rather than returning to live under their thumb. If Cecilia were to be present, I might consider the invitation; but my sister spends the season with her husband's family in York."

He did not like to think of her spending Christmas alone, but he could hardly blame her for refusing her parents' invitation.

"When may I see you again? I do not want to wait another eight years between visits," he said, trying to make a jest out of it. He had to know when he would see her again.

"Cecilia has often invited me to Bath," she said. "I had thought of going there next summer. Not as her guest, of course. I have no wish to be obligated to Lord and Lady Morehead. But it would be pleasant to see her and the children, and to know I have at least one acquaintance there."

Next summer was too far away. It was proper, of course, since only then would her year of mourning be finished. But it was too long for him to wait.

"Lord Grimbley invited me back for the spring

planting," he said. In a way it was true. Lord Grimbley had seemed to enjoy the company of another gentleman farmer and had invited him to return whenever he wished. "If I call on you then, will you receive me?"

Charlotte smiled at him. "I would like that very much. It will give me something to look forward to this winter."

And with that he had to be content.

Charlotte stood in the stableyard, watching as Sweet William was brought out. She was glad that she had finally told Robert everything. After all this time, he deserved to know the truth.

It had shocked her to hear that he had once thought of their marrying. But she had been truthful when she'd said that she would have been a poor wife to him. Back then she had been spoiled and willful. She would have resented his attempts to curb her wild starts. And Robert had a temper of his own, as she knew too well.

They would have fought constantly. Unlike the easygoing George, she did not think that Robert would have left her to her own devices. No, Robert would have insisted on staying with her, until they came to blows or learned to live in harmony.

Robert inspected Sweet William's tack and checked the tightness of the girth. Satisfied with what he found, he came over to make his farewells.

"Write to me, please. And I will see you in the spring," he said. He made a motion as if he would

have embraced her, but then settled for a chaste kiss on the cheek.

He swung up easily in the saddle. He touched his heels lightly to Sweet William's sides. The horse took a few steps forward and then stopped, swinging his head back to look at the stables.

Robert looked confused, but started the horse again. This time Sweet William tried to swing round and head back to his stall.

"What on earth?" Robert said.

"Reckon the horse is just confused," Ben Smith said, glancing warily over toward Charlotte. "Perhaps if I was to lead him?" He advanced toward the horse, but Sweet William began backing up, and then half-reared.

Robert kept his seat easily, but from the set of his face she knew he was confused.

For her part, she had a dreadful suspicion that she knew what was wrong.

"Wait a moment," she said. Crossing to the stable door, sure enough she found Ghost standing in the shadows. "This is all your fault," she whispered.

The kitten looked at her with unblinking eyes, as if proclaiming his innocence. But he allowed her to pick him up and to bring him out into the yard.

Sweet William whickered happily at the sight of his friend. "I am afraid you are going to get more than you bargained for, Robert," she said.

He looked at her, and then at the kitten. "Oh no," he said.

As she approached, the kitten began to squirm in her arms. "Ben, fetch a hamper from the kitchen," she ordered, trying to keep hold of her captive. But Ghost wriggled free and jumped from her arms, landing on Robert's thigh.

"Damn!" Robert swore as the kitten clawed for a safe perch. "Charlotte, this is not at all funny."

But she couldn't help giggling as the kitten settled himself on the saddle between Robert's legs.

"This was not in our agreement."

"I know, but you can see how attached the horse is to him. How much trouble can one little kitten be?"

Robert looked down at the cat and at the damage done to his breeches. "Plenty. This is not a harmless cat. It is a clawing, fur-shedding demon. And you want me to drag him across three counties?"

His breeches would never be the same.

"He will be no trouble at all," she argued. "See, here comes Ben with a hamper to carry him in. He can ride in the carriage and sleep in the stables with Sweet William at night. You will hardly know he is there."

Ben came over and opened the hamper. Robert detached the kitten from the saddle and dropped him into the wicker basket. Ben closed the lid firmly.

"Very well," he said. "But this is it. I don't care how many more strays George left behind."

"You are the kindest of gentlemen." And the wisest. Who knew what Sweet William would have done, had Robert tried to force the horse away from his friend?

The horse watched warily as the hamper was loaded into the traveling carriage.

"I am pleased I brought the carriage," Robert said sarcastically. "The little wretch will find it so much more pleasant than being stuffed in my saddlebag."

"His name is Ghost," she said.

"Why Ghost?"

"Why not?" He would find out soon enough, if Ghost kept up his habit of appearing and disappearing at will. She hoped the kitten had enough sense not to stray too far from Sweet William, lest he become lost during the journey to Robert's home.

"If I did not know better, I would swear that George had somehow planned this," he said.

Charlotte smiled. Indeed, inflicting a kitten on his friend would have appealed very much to George's sense of mischief. But not even George could have manufactured the horse's strange affection for his tiny friend.

"I wish you a pleasant journey," she said.

Robert shook his head then began to grin as he saw the humor of the situation. "Pleasant? Perhaps. But I will wager it is hardly uneventful. Not with this menagerie. But I do thank you for your hospitality. And I wish you well until I see you again."

With that he rode off, taking with him the irascible horse and fierce little kitten who had become the most unlikely of friends. She would miss them. She would miss all of them.

IV

It was after sunset when Sir Robert Harrington arrived in Biddeford. He hadn't planned on traveling in the dark, but the logistics of traveling with a kitten had involved a few unplanned stops. Two of the stops had been to feed the kitten from the jug of cream that Charlotte had thoughtfully provided. The third time the kitten started yowling, he was uninterested in food. Robert finally tucked the kitten into the pocket of his greatcoat, where it promptly curled up and went to sleep.

Ghost was no name for this kitten, he decided. He should be called Yowler, or perhaps simply Pest. But as if to contradict his new name, the kitten gave him no trouble for the rest of the journey.

They stopped at a small inn on the outskirts of Biddeford, where Robert had stayed before. He swung down from the saddle and held the reins of his horse, while his traveling carriage drew up behind him.

There was a brief pause, and then the door to the stables swung open. An old man shuffled out, calling "Who's there?"

Robert bit back a sigh. The inn served a fine meal, but the quality of the stables left much to be desired. The inn had two grooms, old Ned and his grandson known as Little Ned. Robert had been hoping that it would be the energetic Little Ned who came to greet them, rather than his ancient grandsire.

"Sir Robert Harrington," he replied. "You were expecting me."

"Who?"

"Sir Robert Harrington," he yelled.

"No need to shout," the old man said, coming closer and holding up a lantern. He peered into Robert's face. "Ah, I remember you well enough now. But what is a Christian like yourself doing out on a night like this? Don't you know it's not safe? There are wicked spirits abroad."

Robert did not reply. The only spirits that interested him came in a bottle.

The ancient stableman looked over at the carriage and then back at Robert and Sweet William. "There's room for them all in the main barn," he said. "But you needs just wait a bit while I get things ready."

So much for being expected. Robert made a mental note never to patronize this establishment again. No fine meal or well-crafted ale was worth having to stand outside in the chill night air, while the stableman muttered about folks who expected one man to do the work of ten.

"Never mind about this fellow," Robert said as old Ned made a tentative move towards Sweet William. "I will see to him myself. Just help my coachman get the team unhitched and bedded down."

He led Sweet William into the barn and settled him into the first empty stall. Taking off the saddle and bridle, he hung them on the hooks outside the stall, then proceeded to rub the horse down. Sweet William seemed tired after his first long ride in months and gave Robert no trouble. When he was finished he checked the hay and water to make sure that they were fresh. Glancing around he saw a barrel of grain in the corner. Scooping out a generous portion, he filled the horse's manger.

His coat pocket began to rustle and squirm. "I haven't forgotten you, little Ghost" he said, reaching in and pulling out the kitten. He set the kitten down in the straw. The kitten stretched and then promptly stalked off to inspect his new quarters.

"Ghost? Did you say Ghost?" The old man paused, a waterbucket dangling from his hands.

"A cat. The cat is named Ghost." He felt foolish explaining.

The old man gave him a look. "Harumph. If you say so." He was still muttering as he continued down the row of stalls. "Some folks don't know what's good for them. Riding around on All Hallow's, without a sprig of rowan or a cross to protect them. Serve him right if a true ghost came and—"

The old man was still muttering as Robert left the

stables. Jake, his coachman, met him outside and assured him that the team had been bedded down. Satisfied, Robert continued inside.

The innkeeper welcomed him warmly and told him his room had been freshly aired and was ready. After washing up, Robert went downstairs where he indulged himself in a fine dinner and several mugs of their best ale.

But his dreams that night were troubled, no doubt the result of too much rich food. He dreamed of George, not of the youthful friend he had known, but of the man George had become. In his dream George was staring at him, looking gravely disappointed.

"Robbie, you are such a slowtop," the ghostly apparition said. "What will it take for you to see what is right under your nose? Do I have to do everything for you?"

He woke up troubled, and it was some time before he fell back asleep. When he did, his dreams were filled with images of Charlotte, who smiled lovingly at him, but when he reached for her she retreated backwards, always staying just out of his grasp.

He woke, this time covered in sweat. Robert sensed that the dreams were important, but the harder he tried to remember them, the more the details faded, until all he could recall was a sense of sorrow, and of things left undone.

He rose, and opened the shutters. The nearly full moon cut a wide swath across the ground, illuminating it with ghostly brilliance. He felt wide awake, but from the height of the moon he knew it was hours till dawn. Still he stood there, staring, trying to recall what had seemed so clear and important in his dream. Finally the chill drove him back to his bed.

He felt he would never get back to sleep, but he closed his eyes just the same. He was awakened sometime later by a rapping on his door.

"My lord? My lord? You must awake at once."

Robert groaned. The restless night weighed heavily on him. Perhaps if he ignored the shouting, whoever it was would go away.

But the voice was persistent. "My lord? I apologize for the inconvenience, but you really must arise."

Robert threw aside the covers and climbed out of bed. Wrapping a robe around him, he went to the door and unlatched it. "What is it?" he growled.

The portly innkeeper stood there, no longer the affable host of last night, but now pale and sweating. "My lord, I don't know how to say this, I mean nothing like this has ever happened before—"

"Out with it."

The innkeeper met his gaze, and then looked down at the floor again. "Well, um, it seems your horse has gone missing."

"Missing?"

"Well, stolen is more like it," the innkeeper confessed.

"Blast." This trip had been cursed from the start. Nothing had gone right since he had left Torringford. "Give me a moment, and I will be down. And I will want to speak to that incompetent you call a stable man."

"Yes, of course, my lord, and if I may say how much I regret—"

Robert closed the door on the innkeeper's apologies. He did not want to hear how sorry the man was. What he wanted to find out was how something like this had happened.

He dressed swiftly, and as he descended the stairs, he found the innkeeper waiting for him.

Robert looked around, but saw no sign of the old man. "Who discovered the horse was gone?"

"Little Ned. Old Ned's been stable man here since my father's day. Never in all these years has anything like this happened. Why if you ask anyone, they will say that we run an honest establishment—"

Robert went out the front door and headed for the barn. The innkeeper followed along as fast as his bulk would allow.

Jake, his coachman, was waiting outside the barn. "Good morning, Sir Robert," he said. "A terrible thing this is. If I had thought anything was amiss, I would have slept in the barn myself last night."

"It is not your fault." Unlike some employers, Robert didn't expect his coachman to bed down in the stables. A coachman's job was hard enough. "Sweet William is missing. What about the carriage horses?"

"The team is just fine, and the carriage was not disturbed," Jake reported.

Robert nodded and went inside the barn. He was surprised to see that most of the stalls were full, as they had been last night.

Two men were standing inside. The young man, a hulking lad who went by the incongruous name of

Little Ned, seemed calm enough. But his grandfather was clearly ill at ease.

"When did you find Sweet William was missing?" Robert asked.

"He was the big bay horse?" the young man asked. Robert nodded.

"He was here when last eve I came by round eight and told Granda I was going home. But when I came this morning to start the turnout, I found him gone."

So Old Ned had been alone in the stables last night. No wonder he was frightened. He probably assumed, quite rightly, that any blame would fall on his shoulders.

"Are any other horses missing?" Stealing one horse was likely the work of a single man. A band of thieves would have emptied the stable.

"Nay, just the one," the young man said. "But his tack is still here."

Indeed, the saddle was still resting on its stand outside the stall. He should have noticed that himself. Robert looked carefully at the saddle and bridle still hanging on their pegs. Then he looked into the stall. It was empty. Completely empty.

It seemed Ghost had lived up to his name and disappeared as well. He thought a moment, but nothing made sense. How could a stranger get close to Sweet William, a horse with such a notorious temper? Why would anyone take the horse, but leave the valuable saddle behind?

And where had that kitten gone?

An idea occurred to him. It was preposterous, and yet—

"Was the stall door closed when you checked this morning?"

"Yes," said Little Ned.

"No," said the old man.

"No?" Robert asked, his voice deceptively mild.

The old man looked at him, defiance mixing with fear. "It was your fault. You brought him with you."

"Brought whom?"

"The ghost. I heard him last night from my bed." The old man pointed to a door at the end of the barn, where presumably he slept. "I heard the horse call to someone. I came out and there was a man, all misty like. He opened the stall, and then led the horse out to the yard. I followed, but then I saw his face and knew he was no man but an evil ghost. I gave a screech and the ghost looks right at me and says, 'Do not worry, Ned. It will be all right.' Then he rode off. I stood, just a-trembling in my boots for I don't know how long."

Robert had never heard anything more preposterous in his life. "And then? Why didn't you summon help?"

The old man gave him a withering look. "Against a ghost? No man was going to catch that creature, whatever it was. I barred the door and closed the stall back up. Then I stayed put until dawn."

"Ned, you imbecile," the innkeeper shouted.

The grandson merely shook his head in apparent disgust.

"Say what you like, but I know what I know," the old man said stubbornly. "It knew my name, and that was enough for me."

The innkeeper turned to Robert. "I am terribly sorry, my lord. Nothing like this—"

"I know. Nothing like this has ever happened to you before." He found that difficult to believe, given Old Ned's incompetence and credulous nature.

"I could saddle a horse and start searching," Little Ned offered.

"No," Robert refused. "Unless you know where to look, there's no sense in chasing around the countryside." Biddeford sat on a crossroads. There was no way of telling which way the thief had gone. Whoever had taken Sweet William had a clear head start and could be miles away by now.

"If you haven't done so already, I suggest you send for the magistrate."

"Of course, my lord. At once, my lord. Please come inside and let me bring you coffee and a hearty breakfast to make your waiting easier."

The local magistrate, a Mr. Tibbles, arrived later that morning. The magistrate questioned Robert at length, seeming to believe that this must somehow be his fault. After all, nothing like this had happened in Biddeford for years.

The magistrate heard Ned's tale and dismissed it as drink-induced fancy. But he agreed with the innkeeper that it was unlikely that either Ned or his grandson were involved in the theft.

"Gypsies, I tell you it was the gypsies that did it," the innkeeper suggested. "Tom Barrow saw a group of them camped on his land not five days ago."

"I told Tom Barrow to run them off myself," the

magistrate replied. "But they are clever devils and might have gone to ground somewhere else."

This theory seemed to please both the magistrate and innkeeper, exonerating as it did the residents of Biddeford.

"But why would gypsies steal only one horse when they had the chance to steal many?" Robert pointed out.

"Who knows what goes on in their minds? Perhaps they only had time to take the one," Mr. Tibbles reasoned. "I'll send men out to search the woods and notify the magistrates in the surrounding towns to keep a watch for them. If they are still in the county, we'll find them."

Robert thanked the magistrate for his assistance. There was no point in further discussion. The magistrate had made up his own mind as to who the culprits were. And Robert had no better course of action to suggest. He could come to no conclusions himself, but the disappearance of horse and kitten still puzzled him. The only possibility that occurred to him was one that was so ludicrous, he hesitated to voice it aloud.

After the magistrate left, Robert's coachman sought him out. "Sir Robert? I've been thinking about that horse and what might've happened," Jake said.

"Yes?"

"Well he seemed none too eager to leave his home. I got to thinking, what if that old man's tale was half right? What if he was too drunk to close the barn door properly and the horse saw his way free?"

"You think Sweet William bolted back home?"

Jake scratched his head. "I know it sounds crazy, but I've heard of it happening before. The old man probably found the stall empty and invented the ghost story to shift the blame."

"Well, it doesn't sound any less likely than Mr. Tibbles and his gypsies." At least Jake hadn't mentioned the missing kitten. Robert had his own suspicions as to which animal had decided to head for home. The kitten no doubt missed Charlotte, and the horse had already proven he would follow the stupid cat anywhere.

Robert made his decision. "We might as well be doing something, rather than sitting idle," he said. "Hitch up the carriage, and let us retrace our route to Torringford. We can stop along the way to see if anyone remembers seeing the horse. With or without a rider."

It might be a fool's errand, but it was better than waiting around for Mr. Tibbles to take action. If the animals had, indeed, wandered off, how far could one kitten get?

V

Charlotte was in the kitchen garden when Robert arrived, spreading straw with a rake in preparation for winter. He stood for a moment watching her, drinking in the sight of her. She was dressed sensibly, in a faded gray cloak over a black woolen gown. But neither the cloak nor gown could disguise her beauty and her grace.

Then she lifted her head and saw him. She smiled, and the sight of her smile filled him with such gladness that he knew at once what his dreams had been trying to tell him.

"Charlotte," he said simply.

"Robert! Did my messenger find you? I can't tell you how mortified I was when I heard that Sweet William had turned up here this morning."

He didn't care about the horse. "It doesn't matter."

She was still speaking about the horse. "I sent two men after you, but I wasn't sure which road you had taken."

He shook his head. He had encountered no messenger. The fates had been kind, for if he had, he might have turned back to Biddeford. And then he would have missed what waited for him here.

He climbed over the low stone wall and into the kitchen garden. Walking up to Charlotte, he took the rake out of her hands, leaning it carefully against the wall. Then he took her hands in his.

"I swear to you I had no idea he would run away like that," she said.

"That horse has a great deal more sense than you give him credit for. More sense than I," he said.

She stared at him, truly puzzled. "Robert, what are you talking about?" she asked.

He had to speak now, before his courage deserted him. "Charlotte, I've been a fool," he said. "I've made two great mistakes in my life. The first one was eight years ago. The second was yesterday, when I left here without speaking what was in my heart."

She stared at him in rapt attention, giving him strength to continue.

"The other day when I came here with Mr. Osborne, I had another purpose. I came hoping to find that you needed me. It was selfish, I know, but I was hoping that George had left you ill-provided-for. To give me an excuse, a reason for being in your life. But I saw for myself that you were well-provided-for, and needed nothing. So I left."

"Robert—" she began.

He gripped her hands. "Let me finish," he said. He had to say the words now, while his courage held. "I almost spoke yesterday. But I told myself it was too soon. You were still in mourning. I had a dozen reasons why I did not press my suit."

He dropped his eyes, no longer able to bear her gaze. Instead, he fixed his attention on the delicate pulse beating in her neck.

"But the truth is, I was afraid. Afraid that if I asked, you would refuse and then I would have to live without hope. But I can go on like this no longer. I love you. I have always loved you. I need you, and I can not imagine sharing my life with any other woman. Please say that you will take pity on me and be my wife."

He finally dared raise his eyes to hers, and what he read in them kindled the beginnings of hope. His heart, which had held still while he spoke, began to beat once more.

"I have loved you since I was a girl," she said. "But—"

He placed a finger on her lips. "But it is too sudden," he finished for her. "People will talk. They will say that I am no gentleman to come courting so soon."

She nodded. His finger traced her lips and then moved to stroke her cheek.

"It will be a scandal," she said. "I will give my promise today, but we must wait till the year of mourning is over before we call the banns."

He had waited too long already. But Charlotte had been the innocent victim of scandal once before. He would not subject her to that ordeal again. "I do not care what people will say. But if you want us to wait, then I will, for your sake." It was the hardest promise he had ever made.

Charlotte considered him for a long moment. Then she smiled and put her hand on his shoulder. "You were always too noble for your own good," she said. "I suppose if we marry quietly, tongues will wag, but they will soon find something else to talk about."

He grinned, pulling her into his arms.

"I think George would have approved," she said. "All he ever wanted was for me to be happy."

He hugged her tight. "I promise I will do my best to make you very happy," he said.

"I know you will," she replied. Then she tilted her face up towards him, and for the second time in his life Charlotte Makepeace Dawson gave him a kiss. This time he knew he would hold onto her and never let her go.

From his perch on the garden wall, Ghost watched approvingly as the two lovers embraced. He purred to show his satisfaction as he watched Robert holding Charlotte as if she was the dearest thing on earth. Which she was, of course. He should know.

There was only one thing left to do. Leaving the lovers behind, the kitten made his way to the barn, where Sweet William had been stabled following his unexpected arrival. Ghost leaped up to the half door and then stood on the rail facing his friend. The two animals regarded each other solemnly for a moment, and then Sweet William bent his head and lightly touched his nose to Ghost's in salute.

"Mrow," said the kitten, assuring his equine friend that all was, indeed, well. Then in a blink of an eye he disappeared, never to be seen again.

ABOUT THE AUTHOR

Patricia Bray is the author of two Zebra regency romances: A LONDON SEASON and AN UNLIKELY ALLIANCE (now on sale at bookstores everywhere). She loves to hear from her readers and you may write to her c/o Zebra Books. Please include a self-addressed stamped envelope if you wish a response.

LORD TREVOR'S TOMCAT

Cathleen Clare

I

Spring 1816

An eerie wind moaned and whistled around Breakstone House in Mayfair. The gloom of the moonless night seemed to envelope the mansion in a cocoon of lustrous black velvet. Tension growing in the pit of his stomach, Trevor, Lord Breakstone, pushed back from his desk, got to his feet, and crossed the room to his liquor cabinet. Pouring himself a hefty portion of brandy, he closed his eyes against the storm, brought the cool crystal glass to his lips, and drank deeply in hopes that the fiery fluid would somewhat soothe his jangled nerves. But what little ease he gained from the spirits was short-lived. A draft from the rattling window extinguished the brightest candelabrum, plunging the room into ghostly shadow. As the odor of smoking wax reached his nostrils, Trevor gritted his teeth and opened his eyes to the horrible dimness. Heart pounding, he yanked the bell rope to summon a servant, drained his glass, and refilled it.

It seemed like hours, but it was actually only minutes, before his staid butler entered the library. The servant swiftly surveyed the room. "The candles, my lord?" he intoned knowingly.

"Yes." Trevor flushed, realizing that Thorpe must know exactly what was wrong. Despite his potently masculine appearance, no matter his raffish sophistication, regardless of his fine intellect, which told him it was ridiculous, Trevor Breakstone was afraid of storms. The blemish mortified him to no end.

Thorpe hurriedly relit the candles. "Shall I bring more tapers, my lord?"

"If you would. I have difficulty reading in such uncertain light." Feigning nonchalance, Trevor reached up and slipped his forefinger into his neckcloth, loosening its constricting knot. He lowered his gaze and caught the inner flesh of his lip between his teeth, biting down until he felt pain. His humiliation was almost overwhelming.

"I shall return momentarily, sir," the butler assured him and departed.

The marquess polished off his second glass of brandy and poured a third. He wished he didn't have such a head for alcohol. If his level of tolerance had been low, he could have quickly become so intoxicated that he would have blissfully passed out. But that was not to be. Instead, time seemed to drag on to eternity.

Growing impatient for his servant's return, Trevor tried to tell himself that it wasn't much of a storm. There was neither thunder nor lightning. But all the reassurances did no good when the big wind caught a shutter, ripped off its fastener, and banged it shut, nearly causing him to jump out of his skin. When Thorpe calmly reappeared, Trevor could have embraced him.

The butler was laden with as many candles and candlesticks as he could carry. Wordlessly, he set about placing and lighting them in strategic spots around the room. Soon, a comforting glow illuminated the bleakness and even lit up the outside sills of the windows. When he was finished, he executed a half-bow.

"Sir, do you wish refreshments?"

Trevor wasn't hungry, but to prolong the man's attentions and presence, he requested a tray. When the butler left the room, he returned to his desk. He startled as another shutter smashed shut.

It was always best when a storm came in the daytime. The light helped matters, as did the number of staff circulating. At night, the darkness brought forth a menacing element of mystery, and most of the servants were in their rooms, far away from their isolated master.

As a wealthy employer, Trevor could have commanded a few members of his large staff to keep him company at times like this, but he was too ashamed of his phobia to do so. The irrational fear was also the major reason he remained a bachelor, seemingly ignoring his duty to produce an heir. A wife, witnessing such a spectacle as he presented, could never esteem a husband with such an unmanly trait.

He shoved the thought aside and drank heavily once more, barely able to refrain from leaping out of his chair when the wind violently lashed a branch against the windowpane. Would the storm never end? It seemed that it had been going on so very long.

"Christ," he murmured, more in prayer than in profanity.

Thorpe returned, his large silver tray glistening in the candlelight. "You're in luck tonight, my lord."

Good fortune? Trevor could hardly believe that. He raised a questioning eyebrow.

"Cook was up and about, unable to sleep. You'll fare much better than if I had prepared the repast." He set the tray upon the desk and, with a flourish, swept the lid from the platter to reveal a large, hairy spider sitting atop a selection of sandwiches.

"Damn!" Trevor cried and jumped up, overturning his chair. Along with storms, he was ashamed to number arachnids as a phobia, too.

Thorpe, unaware of this fear of his master's, gaped briefly, then slapped at the intruder. The spider hopped lithely to the floor and disappeared. The butler's hand squashed only the sandwiches.

"M'lord, I'm not sure how it got there."

"Got there? Goddamn it! Where did it go now?" Trevor shouted.

The servant winced. "I'll find it, my lord, of that you may be sure!"

Trevor was not at all certain. He retreated to the far end of the room. Turning his back to hide his disgrace, he stared out at the storm. Just as he did so, something black leapt up at him.

"Ya!" The marquess yelped, swore vehemently, and nearly ran from the library.

"It's a cat!" Thorpe hastily assured. "It's only a cat, my lord!"

"What the hell is it doing on my window ledge?" he demanded, heaving a deep breath and blushing deeply.

"Taking refuge from the storm, I'll wager," the butler speculated as a barrage of hail assaulted the glass.

Forcing himself to stand his ground, Trevor snorted. "It can beg help elsewhere. I don't like cats."

"Nor much else, this night," muttered Thorpe.

Clearly hearing the remark, Trevor set his jaw and held back an angry retort. He glared at the cat, which was now brightly illuminated in the glow of the candles. The animal was hunkered down, smited by the driving pebbles of ice, but its glowing yellow eyes did not reveal supplication. Indeed, it stared back at the marquess as if it were on an equal, if not superior, footing with him.

"Bring it inside," Trevor ordered, surprising even himself. "This night's not fit for man nor beast."

"It's just an old, dirty, stray cat, my lord," the butler entreated, "not worthy of a gentleman of your standing."

"I beg to differ," he said sarcastically. "Bring it in. Bring it right here."

"Yes, my lord, but it'll probably flee." Poking out his lip with distaste for his mission, Thorpe abandoned his hunt for the spider and stalked out to do his lordship's bidding.

Momentarily forgetting his twin phobias, Trevor watched with interest as a grimacing footman hove into sight and plucked the cat from its perch, holding it at arm's length and disappearing into the night. Soon the servant reappeared, following Thorpe into the library. The feline squirmed free, jumped from his hands, and took position on the hearth, laving its rough black fur with a long pink tongue.

" 'Tis a witch's familiar," its savior said warily. "Ain't a spot o' white on it."

"It's a disreputable, flea-bitten, alley tomcat," the butler imperiously decreed, twitching his nose. "Look at those chewed-up ears. It's been scrapping."

The marquess grinned lopsidedly. The cat did seem to be a frequent fighter. Aside from its ears, it bore numerous other battle scars.

"Bring him a saucer of milk," he commanded, "and some fish, if there is any."

Thorpe mumbled and cursed, under his breath.

This time, Trevor did not ignore it. "That will be enough, Thorpe. I'm going to keep him," he announced, shifting his gaze from butler to footman, "and there will be no dissension . . . if people value their positions in this household."

The servants exchanged amazed glances.

"Be about it!" Thorpe shoved his minion toward the door. "You heard his lordship."

Disregarding them, the marquess strolled to the

fireplace and sat down, watching with interest as his new pet preened. He was rather astonished that he'd so blithely claimed ownership of the animal. He seldom made such impulsive decisions, but in this case, he hadn't been able to resist. The tomcat humorously reminded him of certain male members of the *ton* . . . a peer named Lord Harris, in particular. The viscount was dark-haired and bore a dueling scar along his jaw near his left ear. Furthermore, he was a roue, prowling about and sparring for feminine favor.

In contrast, Trevor had never known competition. He was handsome, titled, and wealthy enough to make any lady sigh. But he could appreciate the straits of a man like Harris, titled and monied enough, but so physically unattractive that he couldn't seem to bag the type of beautiful woman he so desperately strived to possess. *Lord Harris.* That was the perfect name for his alley cat.

Lord Harris suddenly paused in the licking of a paw. Cocking his head, he intently gaped at a black spot on the carpet in front of him. Swiftly, he batted at it, dragged his claws through the lush pile, and raked forth the now-dead spider. Looking rather self-satisfied, he resumed his grooming.

Trevor chuckled, pleased. "Did you see that, Thorpe?"

"Indeed, sir." The butler strode forward, whipped a handkerchief from his pocket, and plucked up the offensive arachnid.

"He's already earning his keep," the marquess boasted.

Thorpe silently rolled his eyes.

Trevor avidly leaned forward like an excited little boy. "Well, Lord Harris, you've certainly brightened my evening."

"Lord Harris?" his servant queried.

"That shall be his name." He extended his hand and was rewarded by the cat rubbing his jaws against it. "He likes me!"

Abruptly feeling foolish, he straightened. "Of course, I am not overly fond of cats. He isn't a pet. He'll spend most of his time ridding the place of vermin."

"Yes, my lord."

Lord Harris stretched luxuriously, leapt onto the sofa, and settled down to nap.

"He will be valuable."

"Certainly, sir." Smirking, Thorpe lifted the tray. "I shall bring you another serving."

"Thank you." Storm and spider forgotten, Trevor, nevertheless, smiled self-consciously for another reason, his sudden affection for the stray beast.

"Don't forget the milk and fish," he reminded.

"Never, sir." The butler hid a smirk and left the room.

Lord Harris settled into a life of luxury. The alley scrapper had never had it so good. He dined on the freshest fish, which was scrumptiously prepared by a noted French chef. He drank pure, rich cream, delivered post haste straight from the dairy to Lord Breakstone's door. He had his own soft bed in Trevor's chamber, a wicker basket with a pillow stuffed with goose down. And unbeknownst to his master, he slept in the marquess's bed when the spirit moved him. Thus, he was much better off than most cats, but no one could realize it by his appearance.

Lord Harris maintained the disagreeable visage he'd possessed on the night he'd first taken up residence at Breakstone House. In spite of the premier quality and quantity of his foodstuffs, he remained lanky and tube-shaped, with overlong legs and a lengthy, scrawny tail. Usually, whenever Trevor attempted to bathe him, he successfully hid from the marquess and his minions, so his coat remained rough and unkempt. Although he was the pet of a high-ranking peer, he didn't discriminate as to the company he kept. As a result, he was always battered and bitten, and in constant need of first aid. But he pleased Lord Breakstone.

Trevor had never owned a pet. Animals in the house had made his mother sneeze, so he'd never been able to drag in the strays that appealed to the average boy. He'd had hunting dogs when he had grown older, but they had had to live in the kennel, so he'd never developed a close relationship with them. Lord Harris was his first true friend from the animal world. The marquess thought he was wonderful.

Lord Breakstone's servants thought the cat was horrible; moreover, the beast was embarrassing. Lord Harris had a little collar and leash which were to be used whenever he left the confines of the mansion. Other people's servants laughed so hard at the foot-

men who were required to give the cat his exercise
that the men began losing the animal as soon as they
were out of sight of the house, then fibbing to their
master that Lord Harris had slipped his collar and
escaped. The marquess finally gave up on the escorted
excursions and permitted them to let the cat out the
door and leave him to his own devices.

Trevor's best friend, Holland Farwell, held much
the same opinion. Lounging in the library with the
marquess, he spied Lord Harris sitting on the hearth.
"Ye gad, Trev! Where did that thing come from?"

Trevor followed his gaze. "That's my new pet,
Holly. He wandered in one night during a storm."

"You should have let him wander out! That's the
ugliest cat I've ever seen."

He bristled. "I don't find him unattractive."

"Maybe if he were brushed . . ."

"I do groom him . . . whenever possible."

A grin played at the corners of Lord Farwell's
mouth. "You're supposed to brush animals in the
direction of the hair, Trev. Not backwards."

"Do you think I'm an idiot?" Trevor growled. "I
know that."

"Sorry, old boy. You couldn't prove it by the way
he looks. He gives the impression of being a denizen
of London's foulest alleys." He snickered. "Look at
those ears! All scabs and scars. And what is that greasy
substance crowning them?"

"It's salve," the marquess said tightly.

"Ah-hoo! Been fighting for feminine, feline favors,
has he?" The viscount shouted with laughter. "No
wonder! No self-respecting lady cat would willingly

come his way. He's so unsightly, I'll wager that he has to sneak up on a saucer to get a drink of milk!''

"That will be enough, Holly. I happen to like Lord Harris.''

"Lord Harris?" His friend laughed all the louder. "Now that's an apt name for an ill-favored, female-chasing knave!''

Trevor rose angrily.

Lord Farwell looked up, smile fading. "Good God, you aren't going to call me out, are you?''

"Maybe I should. I've had just about all I can bear of your insults, Holly,'' he warned. "That cat is my pet. He means a great deal to me. Your disparagement of him equals contempt for me.''

"Oh, for God's sake! Sit down, Trev. You know you're my dearest confrere!'' he professed. "I'm merely jesting about the cat. Your having a pet is just so surprising.''

"I suppose it is,'' Trevor allowed, but instead of claiming his chair, he walked to the hearth and swooped up Lord Harris into his arms. He admitted to himself that he was being rather foolish over the beast, but dammit! He did enjoy the cat's company!

"If you're starved for affection, my friend,'' he heard Holly murmur, "you'd be better served by taking a wife.''

"Fustian!'' Sophie Markwell reached for a weapon, which turned out to be merely a hunk of fallen, rotting bough. With all her might, she hurled it ineffectively after the devilish, black tomcat. "Begone, you foul beast! Scram!"

The cat lithely darted away, leapt onto the boundary wall, and sat, eyeing her with a supercilious grin and negligently licking a paw.

"Go away and never come back!" She made a run at the animal, smacking her feet hard on the ground in a futile attempt to frighten it. "You horrid, unwelcome creature!"

If the tom had been human, he would have drawn his nose in arrogance. As it was, he made an excellent feline facsimile of it, then turned and aloofly leapt from sight into the neighboring backyard.

The young lady made a face at him and uttered a most unladylike curse, which would have shocked her vicar father beyond all belief. "And you ..." She turned to see her gray tabby emerge from the shubbery, looking terribly sated and well-satisfied. "Have you no morals at all, Lady Jane?"

The cat approached to rub against her ankles.

Sophie sighed. "Oh, how did you contrive to escape from the house this time? If you are in the family way, I just don't know what I shall do! It was difficult enough to find homes for your previous brood. Well, perhaps I can be successful just one more time. After all, I have made new friends here in London."

"Uh ... ma'am," the feeble voice of her Aunt Bess's elderly gardener emanated from behind a boxwood hedge. "There's ... uh ... probably gonna be kittens."

She set her jaw and reached down to pick up the naughty tabby. "What luck!" she muttered, walking toward the house. "Especially after I had to expend all my wits cajoling Aunt Bess into allowing me to bring you to town. Goodness, Lady Jane! Now what shall we tell her?"

Her ill temper increased with every stride. Aunt Bess had been very outspoken concerning her prejudice against female cats. Now, because of this tragedy, the proud Sophie would have to beg mercy. By the time she reached the kitchen door, she was nearly blind with fury. She set Lady Jane on the floor inside.

"Cook, please do *not* allow my cat to get out. I shall be back for her shortly," she requested and returned to the yard. "I will complain to the neighbors, that's what I'll do! And they *will* assist in finding homes for the kittens. After all, they are fifty-percent responsible!"

She stalked toward the walkway, which led past the side of the house to the street. From the corner of her eye, she caught a movement and turned to see the dastardly black tomcat spring onto a trellis. "Aha! Back again? I've got you now!"

She quietly strolled up to him and, with a lightning motion, plucked him from his perch. Surprisingly, the cat did not resist, merely hanging limply in her hands. Holding his dirty body at arm's length, she carried him to the neighboring house, wondering what kind of people would keep such a disgusting pet.

The butler must have seen her coming for he opened the door before she set foot on the stoop.

"I wish to speak with the owner of this aggravating

animal," she said imperiously. "I have a very serious complaint to lodge."

The butler frowned, not angrily, but with concern. "Well, miss, uh . . ."

"I am Miss Sophie Markwell, from next door." She tossed her head. "Announce me, and be quick about it."

"But, miss, it isn't . . ." He reached for the bundle in her hands. "I'll take the cat and relate any . . ."

"I insist upon seeing this ugly beast's owner!" She drew the tomcat out of his reach. "I will do so if I have to search this entire house for the proper person."

He winced, motioning her in. "One moment, please."

"Be hasty." She nodded curtly, entering. "This cat is guilty of creating a holocaust on my aunt's property, and I intend to receive satisfaction."

"Yes, miss." He fled down the hall.

Distrusting him, Sophie followed. The servant might grant her lip service while protecting his employer from her ire. She would simply not allow it. She would see the tomcat's warden! No butler, however dexterous, would deter her. Lips pressed tightly together in a fine line of irritation, she entered the room where the man had gone and . . .

Sophie nearly gasped. Regarding her with shocked, dark-lashed, blue eyes was the handsomest man she had ever seen in all her lifetime. Her knees and her arms seemed to turn to water. It was all she could do to avoid dropping the cat.

"Miss Markwell!" the butler announced. "From next door. My lord."

The paragon rose and came 'round his desk, bowing. "May I be of assistance, Miss Markwell?"

"I hope so," she managed. "You are . . ."

"Breakstone," he supplied, sweeping his gaze from her head to her toes. "We are neighbors?"

She nodded, too breathless to speak. Her mind spun with scraps of recollections. She'd heard of Lord Breakstone. He was a marquess who moved in the finest circles. Rumor had it that he was a dedicated bachelor. And of course, everyone mentioned how handsome he was, but she never would have imagined he would be like *this*. He was a veritable god.

Almost simultaneously, as she catalogued his attributes, she took stock of her own . . . or more explicitly, her lack thereof. Sophie was not pretty, and she did not need a looking glass to tell her so. She could read it in the manner in which people glanced at her, then looked away in dismissal. It was demonstrated by the gentlemen who chose to be her dancing partners in this, her first season. They were the homely, pimply faced youths, not potentially serious suitors.

Her one pretty feature was her hair, which was a long, silky, and richly hued auburn. Unfortunately, she was forced by the current mode to bob it or contain it. If she could have allowed it to stream gloriously over her shoulders, she might have garnered some male attention. But that was not to be done. Therefore, she must resign herself to being a spinster, when she wanted so desperately to have a husband and children to love.

Recognizing her status in life re-ignited her anger and gave her the courage to confront His Most Handsome Lordship. She abruptly poked the cat toward him. "Does this beast belong to you?"

His beautiful eyes danced with amusement. He faintly smiled. "I suppose I must admit to ownership."

"Then, here!" She gently tossed the tom toward him.

Recoiling with surprise, Lord Breakstone still deftly managed to catch his pet. "Good God, girl! He could have fallen and hurt himself!"

"I seriously doubt that! Your cat is the most agile feline I've ever seen. You should witness his leaps to and from high walls," she snapped. "He is creating havoc on my aunt's property. He must be contained or . . . or I will shoot!"

Lord Breakstone's humor returned. He bit his lower lip in an attempt to prevent a muffled chuckle.

"This is not a laughing matter, Lord Breakstone," she admonished. "I demand satisfaction!"

"That is serious, indeed," he said, but a grin still threatened to curve his lips.

Of all unfair advantages, he had dimples! The sight of those attractive holes in his cheeks rendered her momentarily speechless. She could only glare at him.

Tucking his cat against his shoulder, he gestured toward a chair. "You shouldn't be here, but since you are, perhaps you'd best be seated, Miss Markwell. Thorpe, please bring us refreshments."

"Yes, my lord." The butler glanced with hard disapproval at Sophie and departed, conspicuously leaving the door wide open.

"You will sit down?" Lord Breakstone asked more kindly. "This sounds like serious business."

He still looked as if he were trifling with her. It angered her to no end. Suddenly, she was glad she was plain. She needn't attempt to be charming in hopes of gaining his favor. She could tell the marquess exactly what she thought!

She seated herself, decorously smoothing her skirts in a ruse of stalling for time so that she might conjure the grandest setdown in history.

Lord Breakstone deposited his cat on a pillow by the hearth, brushed dust from his coat, then settled himself in a chair opposite her. "Do enlighten me, Miss Markwell, on what Harris has done to incite your wrath."

She inquisitively tilted her head. "Harris?"

"My cat. His name is Lord Harris."

Having been introduced to the human Lord Harris and watching his capers, Sophie found herself sucking in her cheeks in an effort to maintain her indignant demeanor. She lifted her chin and pursed her lips. "I do not care what he is called. I merely want him to mind his own business."

"And of what heinous act is he guilty?"

"Well . . ." In the heat of her anger, Sophie hadn't considered that she might have to detail the tomcat's exploits.

"Well . . ." she began again. "He stepped on my aunt's flowers. And that is not all!"

"My goodness," he drawled. "I wonder if I can contemplate more than one crime per day."

"Do not make light of it, Lord Breakstone," she

hissed. "Duels have been fought for less provocation!"

He lifted an eyebrow and chuckled. "Are you calling me out, Miss Markwell?"

She gritted her teeth. "I should."

"A lady challenging a gentleman?" He merrily shook his head. "No, no, that wouldn't do. Chivalry would demand that I delope. Then you would undoubtedly shoot me dead. No, Miss Markwell, I prefer to make amends. After we finish our refreshments, perhaps you will take me to the scene of the crime. Now, pray tell, what other offense did my cat commit?"

Thinking of what she intended to relate, Sophie felt as if her whole body had burst into flames. This hadn't been a good idea. In fact, it had been a perfectly awful one. She searched her brain for a way to get out of this confrontation and out of his house. What a fool she had been!

"Miss Markwell?" he prompted.

She bit her lip.

All humor faded from Lord Breakstone's face. "You haven't come here in hopes of compromising me, have you?"

"You . . . You knave!" she cried, snapping from her state of shock. "How dare you accuse me of that!"

"Frankly, it is a distinct possibility. Why else would a spinster call on a bachelor?"

"That is not the truth!" She bounded to her feet. This allegation, on top of her prior discomfort, was too mortifying to bear. She could only think of escape. Blindly, she dashed to the nearest exit, a set of French doors that overlooked Lord Breakstone's rear garden. Wrenching them open, she got up the nerve to fire a final salvo.

"Your Lord Harris caused *my* Lady Jane to be in a family way, and you must share the responsibility!"

The marquess shouted with laughter.

"You are as deplorable as that ugly beast you harbor!" she called over her shoulder as she ran outside. Searching rapidly for an exit, she unproductively charged off in several different directions, but failed to find an outlet. There must be a gate somewhere! It was probably hidden within the shrubbery, and she was just too panicked to see it. Glancing back at the house, she spied Lord Breakstone leaning negligently in the doorway, arms and legs crossed, and grinning broadly.

"Oh, damn!" she breathed. "He knows I am trapped!"

Sophie refused to give the marquess the satisfaction of witnessing her defeat. Whirling, she saw a rose trellis standing by the wall which probably marched with the alley. Rushing to it, she began to climb.

Luckily, the rose plant was small and bore only short canes to impede her progress. In the beginning, she received only minor scratches, but disaster struck when she tried to scramble onto the top of the barrier. Her skirts bound her legs, holding her immovable. Before she could make an adjustment, there was a terrible crack as her makeshift ladder broke off at the ground and began to topple. As if that were not enough, a side seam in her dress gave way, exposing her left limb from its shapely thigh to its neatly turned ankle. Faint with horror, Sophie grabbed for the top of the wall and kicked free of the trellis, hoping to shinny her way to freedom. But her precarious hold had begun to slip when strong arms caught her and drew her downward. With smothering humiliation, she gazed at her naked leg, and then at Lord Breakstone's breathtaking face.

"Let me down!" she shrilled.

"I am attempting to do so."

He seemed to take an inordinately long time to return her to the ground, and all the while he stared fixedly at her bare limb.

"I have never been so mortified!" Sophie wailed, blessedly finding her balance on the firm ground. Impulsively, she drew back her hand and smacked his face.

"Damn!" cried the marquess, holding his cheek. "What was that for? Is that what I deserve for saving you from a nasty fall?"

"You know what it's for," she accused, trying to hold her dress fabric together.

"It isn't my fault that you ripped your gown," he defended. "I was merely trying to be a gentleman."

"Gentleman, ha! You didn't have to look! Now leave me alone!" Abruptly, she took to her heels again, this time running toward the house.

Briefly stunned, the marquess hastened after her.

With a good lead on him, Sophie entered the library and fled into the hall.

"Wait!" shouted Lord Breakstone. "You can't go out like that!"

She ignored him, bolting toward the front door.

She passed the butler, who yelped and dropped his big silver tray of refreshments with a loud clatter. A housemaid gaped and leapt from her path. Two avidly ogling footmen were so entranced that they were unable to tend the door. Sophie herself wrenched it open and exited.

"No!" the marquess blared.

At the property on the other side of Lord Breakstone's dwelling, the grand gossip, Lady Hawthorne, was gliding toward her carriage. She took one look, gawked, and fumbled for her lorgnette. Peering again, she crumpled into a dead faint.

Sophie glimpsed her from the corner of her eye and increased her pace, hoping the old witch hadn't recognized her. She then looked round at Lord Breakstone, who had given up pursuit of her and was sprinting back into his home, no doubt hoping the same. Skirt flapping appallingly, Sophie reached her aunt's residence and nearly fell through the portal.

Her Aunt Bess, halfway up the stairs, paused in open-mouthed shock. "What on earth has happened to you?"

Sophie struggled for breath. "Lord Breakstone," she forced out.

"He assaulted you?" the lady cried.

"No, I was fleeing over his back wall and . . ." Her head reeled. She looked down with horror at her tattered gown. "Dear Lord, I wish I were dead!"

Sophie, enswathed in her cozy dressing robe, sat curled up in her bedchamber's window seat, sipping a most welcome glass of sherry. Aunt Bess sat in a chair beside her, her own drink in her hand. Totally ignoring them both, Lady Jane innocently lay in the center of Sophie's bed, grooming herself with a rough, pink tongue.

Sophie sadly eyed her cat. "Oh, Lady Jane, if only you hadn't escaped the house."

She knew, even before the words left her mouth, that her predicament was not the tabby's fault. She had used poor judgment. Now, she must live with it.

Aunt Bess leaned forward. "Let us go over it once more."

Sophie hung her head. "Must we? It will alter nothing."

"Are you certain you haven't left something out? Think, my dear. Perhaps you exaggerated. Maybe you have forgotten an important point that will make all the difference." She hopefully arched a brow, studied her niece's face, then regretfully answered her own question. "No. Then we must accept the facts that we have."

She nibbled a nail. "What is the worst that could happen?"

Her aunt grimaced. "This is painful. . . . If worse becomes worst, Sophie, you will have to go home. In disgrace, I fear."

Sophie could feel her cheeks flush in anticipation of it. Her parents would be very disappointed and terribly mortified. Her father, a vicar, would be particularly embarrassed, because his whole parish would be sure to ferret out what had happened.

"Your only hope," Aunt Bess continued, "is that Lady Hawthorne did not identify you."

"And that Lord Breakstone holds his tongue," she added.

"I am not concerned about the marquess. Lord Breakstone is a gentleman. There has never been a particle of gossip circulated about him."

"There will be now," Sophie predicted.

Her aunt shrugged. "Yes, and he will have to live with it. No doubt, he will be angry, but he won't blame you. Not publicly, that is."

"But it is my fault. I shouldn't blame him for tattling."

"Don't expect him to do that! If he did, he would be forced to wed you. You were compromised, you know."

Sophie blushed, remembering how Lord Breakstone had accused her of compromising him. Well, albeit through no prior plotting, she had done just that.

Lady Nay frowned thoughtfully. "Upon further reflection, I believe we should discuss the circumstance with Lord Breakstone. We shouldn't be left guessing as to what plan of defense he might make. We'll invite him to dinner."

"No!" wailed Sophie. "I cannot face him again! It would be much too mortifying."

"You will contrive," her aunt said confidently.

"No," she begged. "Please do not ask me to meet him again!"

Aunt Bess ignored her plea. "Yes, that will be the

best thing to do. I shall write him immediately, for our plan of action must not wait."

Sophie clenched her hands so tightly together that her nails bit into her flesh. With a hopeless sigh, she watched her aunt flutter from the room. Lady Nay might shrug off her niece's ability to rise to the occasion. She was accustomed to High Society. But the inexperienced Sophie wondered how on earth she would face the sophisticated man-about-town. Just thinking about it made her stomach knot.

She gazed from the window, which overlooked the marquess's garden. There was a torn piece of her white petticoat hanging boldly from the demolished trellis. Groaning, she buried her face in her voluminous dressing gown and wept with mortification.

The spectacle of Lady Hawthorne's ghastly expression haunted Trevor's memory for hours after the *cat debacle,* as he termed the scandalous episode. That loose-tongued, crotchety, old tattle-monger had certainly gotten an eyeful today. At her age, her eyesight might be rather poor, but truly she should have seen enough to play judge, jury, and executioner to himself and Miss Markwell. The fact that the young lady had entered his home was enough to convict. Her departure, torn gown and all, was enough to bring down the social wrath of all England upon their heads. How to avoid this social crime? There was no way! How to lessen the capital sentence? Marriage!

Trevor shuddered, halting his pacing. Oh no, not that! Lord, deliver him! He wasn't ready for wedlock.

Moreover, he was scarcely acquainted with Miss Markwell. Then there were his outrageous phobias to consider. Miss Markwell acted as if she were not afraid of anything. She'd despise and laugh at him if she knew of his damnable weaknesses. With a moan of protest, he continued his march back and forth across the library floor.

Before he had made many more passes, Thorpe scratched on the door and entered. "Lord and Lady Hawthorne have come calling, my lord."

"Oh, God." Trevor cursed under his breath. "Tell them I'm ill. Tell them I'm out. Tell them anything! Just get rid of them."

"For shame, Lord Breakstone," Lady Hawthorne scolded in her high, forceful voice as she stepped from behind the butler. "Do not attempt to escape."

Trevor cringed.

"If it were not for your dear, departed mama, I would not set foot in this den of iniquity," she stated, forging ahead with her long-suffering husband trailing after her. "But, alas, I must do my duty to her cherished memory."

"And what is that?" he asked perversely.

She reared back her head, nostrils flared, in a magnificent imitation of a dragon breathing fire. Trevor couldn't help himself. He laughed aloud.

She grew red in the face. "Now, see here, young man!"

Lord Hawthorne took her elbow and tried to steer her to the hall. "Come along, Hyacinth, let us be on our way. You have registered your disapproval. Now let us allow Lord Breakstone his privacy."

"Shut up, Donald!" she retorted. "I have come here for a purpose, and I intend to dispense it. Let me go!"

Trevor pointedly eyed Lord Hawthorne. "Do come in. Would you care for refreshments? A glass of brandy, perhaps?"

"Yes," said the elder man gratefully, dropping his hand from his spouse's arm.

"No," said his wife. She paraded toward the sofa, great hips churning. Plopping down, she glared at the gentlemen.

Trevor signaled Thorpe to prepare drinks and wearily gestured Lord Hawthorne to take a seat.

"This is a terrible situation," the lady commenced. "I shall go right to the point with no sparkling preamble. After what has taken place, Lord Breakstone, you must wed Miss Markwell. There is no other remedy. That is what your mama, my best-ever friend, would have wished."

"I'm not so sure about that," Trevor remarked. "Not if she were acquainted with all the facts."

Lady Hawthorne eagerly leaned forward. Just what are they?"

He searched for an answer that would put both himself and Miss Markwell in the clear. As he did so, he spied Lord Harris lying on his cushion by the hearth. "Miss Markwell kindly returned my missing cat. That is all."

"Huh!" she snorted. "With her clothing all asunder?"

"A great misfortune." He thankfully accepted a

beaker of brandy and drank deeply. "Cat's claws, don't you know."

"No, I *don't* know." Her eyes glittered suspiciously. "I have never seen a cat inflict such damage."

"My cat had a deplorable past . . . scrapping in alleys and the like. He is an accomplished combatant."

"I still don't believe that a little cat could tear a gel's skirt from waist to hem." She stared at Lord Harris. "That is the ugliest cat I've ever seen, Breakstone."

"The poor thing was a stray," he said, hoping to arouse her sympathy. "I took him in out of pity."

Apparently, Lady Hawthorne was not an animal lover. "You should have wrung his neck and put him out of his misery. If you wanted a cat, you'd have done better to find one of pedigree. Furthermore, I wonder if that is the black cat my gardener has been complaining about. The beast is creating all sort of havoc in my flower beds."

"My cat never leaves the house without supervision, madam."

"No?" She narrowed her eyes. "Then why was Miss Markwell returning it?"

Trevor mentally flogged himself. "Well . . . ah . . . he escaped!"

"You may as well know that I do not trust a word you say, young man."

Her husband downed his brandy and rose. "Let us be on our way, Hyacinth. You have demonstrated your concern for Lord Breakstone's reputation. Now we'll leave."

"No. Not until he promises to do the honorable thing," she vowed. "I owe it to his mama!"

"You have discharged your debt." Hawthorne reached for her hand.

She batted him away. "Lord Breakstone, will you wed Miss Markwell?"

"I will not," he declared. "There is no reason for it."

"Oh, yes, there is! The reputation of you both will be ruined."

Trevor stubbornly stuck out his chin. "Only if gossip is circulated, Lady Hawthorne."

She fidgeted. "Surely you do not think that *I . . .*"

He gazed coolly at her.

"I assure you," she stuttered, "that I am not a tattler! But there are servants involved . . . and passersby on the street."

"My servants will remain silent," he told her, "and there were no other people on the streets at that time."

"Ha!" she sniffed. "You will find that you cannot depend upon servants to hold their tongues. *You must wed Miss Markwell.* That is the only solution. Furthermore, it's time that you set up your nursery."

"Hyacinth!" cried her husband. "This is not your affair! Now I am leaving whether you do or not. I won't be a party to this any longer!"

Begrudgingly the countess stood. "Mark my words, Breakstone. If you do not wed the chit, you will join the ranks of the blackest rakes and Miss Markwell will be ruined."

Trevor gritted his teeth to avoid cursing at her. She

planned to gossip, and she'd blame it on the servants. Barely keeping his temper in check, he escorted the couple to the door.

Lady Hawthorne sailed forth, but her lord hung back. "I'm as sorry as I can be, Breakstone. But I can't control her. Hyacinth always did have a mind of her own."

Trevor raised a shoulder, but he did not reassure the man. If he couldn't restrain his own wife, he should have kept her hidden away in the country. Now she'd spread scandal, and her husband wouldn't lift a finger to stop her, shielding himself by his excuse. And whose fault was this predicament? Miss Markwell's!

Gritting his teeth, Trevor again sought his library. He scowled at Harris.

The cat yawned and stretched, oblivious to his role in the drama.

"It's your fault, too," the marquess accused. "It was a sorry night when I took you in."

The tomcat arose and sauntered over to him, rubbing his lanky body on Trevor's legs.

"I won't forgive you," Trevor warned.

Harris mewed.

"Rascal." Shaking his head, he picked up the animal and scratched his ears. "You've gotten me into a miserable situation, you know. Have you been scheming with Miss Markwell? Are you part of an intricate plot to trap me in marriage?"

The cat eyed him blankly.

"Why don't you think of a way to get me out of it?" Trevor placed the cat on his desk and sat down, plunging into some paperwork to help take his mind from the dilemma. He scarcely heard Thorpe when the man entered.

"A message for you, sir."

Trevor broke the seal and immediately looked at the signature. *Lady Nay.* Now, more trouble was starting.

"What if he does not come?" Sophie shifted uncomfortably in her chair in the drawing room. She had dressed with great care for the occasion, choosing a cream-colored, low-cut gown trimmed in mint-green flowers. Her hair was done up in a high knot with loose tendrils framing her face. Although it was positively scandalous, she had, secretly, touched her cheeks and lips with Aunt Bess's rouge to hide the pallidness caused by her overset nerves. All in all, she decided she looked as well as a plain girl could hope to do.

"What if he does not come?" she repeated more loudly.

This time, her aunt heard. "He will attend. After all, he did accept the invitation."

"He might have had a change of heart."

"No, he'll be here. You may depend upon it." She laughed lightly. "Lord Breakstone's cat might not be a gentleman, but its master is. You may have a low opinion of him, Sophie, but the marquess is quite a fine young man."

Her niece made a moue of distaste.

"By the way," Lady Nay continued, "I must compliment you on your appearance. You look quite lovely, Sophie.''

She couldn't help chuckling. "Really, Aunt, I could never look lovely. Neatness is the highest acclaim to which I could aspire.''

"I must take exception to that observation. I think you look pretty, even though your color is a bit high.''

Sophie bent her head to avoid her gaze. "I am greatly overset.''

"Of course.'' Aunt Bess lightly patted her shoulder. "But I believe that all will go well.''

The heavy door knocker fell, sending Sophie's nerves into a flurry. He had arrived. She demurely folded her hands, but clenched her fingers together almost painfully. She was as mortified as anyone could ever dream of being. What would she say to him?

"Lord Breakstone,'' the butler announced.

Lady Nay rose and smilingly greeted him. "How kind of you to come, my lord.''

"So nice of you to invite me.''

Standing, Sophie bit her lip in frustration. How could they exchange mundane pleasantries when the earth itself was shattering? It was simply awful!

"Miss Markwell.'' The marquess's voice seemed slightly chilly as he bent over her hand.

"How do you do, Lord Breakstone?'' she managed.

Thankfully, he did not reply. If he had, the comeback would probably have been devastating. She was the one who had thrust him into this hideous quandary. Most likely, he hated her. He had good reason to do so.

Still avoiding so much as looking at him, she seated

herself and studied her hands. Her thoughts whirled. What could she say to him? Nothing! She'd best leave the discourse to Aunt Bess.

Preprandial drinks were served, and the butler departed. Silence reigned. It seemed like hours before Aunt Bess spoke.

"We find ourselves plunged into a sticky dilemma, do we not, my lord?"

The marquess sighed. "It would seem so."

"Of course, we just might be lucky enough to discover that my niece went unrecognized," she said hopefully.

"I'm sorry to say that good fortune eluded us," he mildly proclaimed. "I've had a visit from Lady Hawthorne. She saw and recognized Miss Markwell. There was no doubt in her mind."

Sophie looked up helplessly. "I shall return home at once."

Lord Breakstone shrugged. "Do what you will. It makes no difference to me. Unfortunately, I cannot run from the problem."

His self-sacrificing attitude incited Sophie's ire. "I realize, Lord Breakstone, that the fault is mine; but you needn't act like such a woeful martyr."

His eyes flashed. "I was not aware I was giving that impression; but, indeed, I have every right to act like the injured party. You took your own reputation in your hands, madam. I don't appreciate your taking mine."

"And I thought you were a gentleman," she scoffed.

"Let us not quarrel," Lady Nay broke in. "That will benefit no one."

Lord Breakstone smirked. "No, but it will provide some satisfaction."

Sophie wrinkled her nose, but held her tongue.

"There must be a way to salvage both reputations," her aunt mused.

Lord Breakstone sneered. "Marriage."

"Well, I certainly have no desire to marry you," Sophie pronounced.

"My sentiments exactly," he retorted.

"Please!" Lady Nay threw up her hands. "Do be civil."

Exchanging rejoinders with him had a remarkable way of easing Sophie's anxiety. She found, however, that looking at him had precisely the opposite effect. Lord Breakstone was as handsome as she remembered him to be, if not more so. If only she could have a tiny portion of his good looks! It wasn't fair that he'd been born a Greek god and she, a plain, simple dove.

"There, now." Her aunt nodded, pleased with the silence. "Let us begin once more."

Lord Breakstone inclined his head in assent.

"Sophie?"

"Aunt, you know I am willing to do whatever I must to save everyone from total dishonor."

The marquess chuckled without humor. "Everything except marriage."

"My lord, this is not a laughing matter," Sophie said scornfully. "I wish you would cease mocking me."

Aunt Bess interrupted. "I wonder how much Lady Hawthorne actually saw."

"Most everything, I would guess." Lord Breakstone cleared his throat. "She was well aware of Miss Markwell's torn gown."

"I wonder," pondered Lady Nay, "if I went to Lady Hawthorne and cast myself upon her mercy . . ."

"Don't ignoble yourself, my lady," Lord Breakstone advised. "Given the woman's reputation for gossip, I have no reason to believe that she will hold her tongue under any circumstances. No doubt, she would only add your visit to her recitation."

Sophie's aunt sighed unhappily. "Yes, I suppose there is no hope. She will bruit it abroad to as many people as will listen."

Sophie sipped her ratafia. There was no neat solution, other than marriage, and that certainly wouldn't do. She could just picture herself as Lord Breakstone's wife. Marriage to him would only bring heartache. He could never come to love her, not with so many beautiful women casting themselves in his path.

"Let us explore all other options," Aunt Bess decided. "Of course, marriage . . ."

". . . is impossible," the marquess finished. "It is obvious that your niece does not wish to marry me. Therefore, I do not believe we should consider marriage as one of our options."

Sophie piercingly studied him, attempting to witness some sign of repugnance, but there was none. Lord Breakstone was inscrutable. It was vastly aggravating.

"I daresay you could jump for joy at that conclusion, my lord," she said caustically.

"Not at all," he returned. "My, but you must have a low opinion of your charms, Miss Markwell."

She wished she could fly up and strike his benign face. "I am modest. That trait is far preferable to an overinflated view of oneself."

"Neither extreme is admirable."

"I beg to differ. Modesty is next to godliness."

A smile tugged at the corners of his mouth. His dimples deepened. "Hm, I thought it was *'Cleanliness is next the Godliness.'* "

"That is correct, Lord Breakstone," Aunt Bess agreed.

Sophie's cheeks burned. "Nevertheless, modesty is to be celebrated."

"Not be me," the marquess said in an annoyingly teasing voice. "I prize honesty above all else."

"That is because there is not a modest bone in your body," Sophie stated.

He allowed the slow grin to take possession of his lips. "So, the kitten flexes her claws again. I am fair bewitched."

"Fiddlesticks!"

This time, Aunt Bess did not attempt to silence their squabble. Instead, she glanced back and forth with interest. In her eyes was a very speculative expression. Sophie highly distrusted it. Surely her aunt did not intend to push the idea of marriage. That just wouldn't fadge.

She was assuaged when the butler chose that moment to announce dinner. Lord Breakstone

offered Aunt Bess his arm, and the two proceeded
from the parlour. Sophie trailed behind, unable to
keep from staring at the marquess's exquisite figure.
From head to foot, he was just about perfect. What
would it be like to be wed to such a paragon? Alas,
she would never know. If she were beautiful, her
tiny dowry might be of no consequence. If she were
wealthy, her plainness might not be an obstacle. As
it was, few gentlemen, if any, would wish to wed a
poor, unattractive young lady. Maybe she should simply forget attempting to salvage some sort of honor
and go home.

As the meal progressed, she slowly relinquished
her pride and became convinced that retreat was the
best solution. When they returned to the parlour for
coffee, she voiced her opinion. "Frankly, Aunt Bess,
I believe it would be best for me to return to the
country."

"What?" Lady Nay cried out.

"I shall go home. Once there, I shall actively pursue
a post as a governess. I have always desired to work
with children."

Lord Breakstone had the audacity to laugh.

"I won't hear of it," Aunt Bess said unequivocally.

"No one will hire you," the marquess maintained.

She frowned. "I don't see why not! My father edu-
cated me far beyond what is usual for a female. I am
eminently suited to teach."

"You are not. You're too attractive, Miss Markwell.
No woman will hire you."

"Oh . . . oh!" she gasped. "Why must you make
fun of me?"

"He isn't," insisted her aunt. "Now, listen to me, Sophie. Here is a possible solution, if Lord Breakstone will agree."

He eyed her warily. "That depends on what it is."

"I think you will like my idea, my lord." Aunt Bess nodded eagerly. "It is as simple as this. We shall *pretend* that the two of you are engaged. You will escort Sophie to social events, for drives in the park, and so on. Insofar as the encounter in question, we'll simply answer Lady Hawthorne's accusations by saying that Sophie unwisely went to your house to return the cat and that the beast tore her skirt. It will be entirely believable. With Sophie being new to London manners, she will have thought that her visit to your house was permissible, since the two of you were to be wed."

Sophie lowered her gaze. Lord Breakstone as escort and hovering fiance? Her heart made a funny thump.

"At the end of the Season, we'll announce that the engagement is broken by mutual consent," her aunt continued. "Of course, the plan does have its drawbacks. Both of you will have lost that time in seeking a spouse."

A ponderous silence fell. Sophie looked through her long, thick eyelashes at her aunt. Lady Nay was waiting anxiously for Lord Breakstone's reply, a curiously sparkling and mischievous expression on her face. She shifted her regard to the marquess. He was frowning.

"I am not searching for a bride at the moment," he related hesitantly. "If I took part in this ruse, the biddies would assume I was in the market for a spouse.

When Miss Markwell dumps me, they'll consider me fair game for another wifely candidate. They'll pursue me relentlessly."

Aunt Bess's countenance resumed its sophisticated control. "Then your answer is *no?*"

"I fear that it must be. You do understand?" He had the grace to smile apologetically at Sophie. "Nothing personal, you know."

An inexplicable surge of disappointment swept over her. Despite her initial irritation with Lord Breakstone, it might have been fun to pretend that she was his chosen mate. But it was probably best that the plot had not transpired. After all, falsehood seldom prevailed. They might have been caught in the scheme.

Lord Breakstone continued to smile questioningly, waiting for her to requite him. She managed to smile in return.

"I know, my lord." Although she'd intended neutrality, the simple statement sounded heavy with underlying meaning.

He lifted an eyebrow.

"I am not your type. The deception would be far too obvious. Now, if you will excuse me?" She rose. "The tension has been great, and I am weary to the bone."

Before the marquess could politely rise, Sophie walked swiftly from the room.

II

Trevor left Lady Nay's house with a small, nagging sense of guilt, although why he should feel such a sentiment, he could not understand. All the responsibility for the incident leading to Miss Sophie Markwell's ruination lay on her own head. He was totally innocent. *He* had not caused her impropriety in coming to his home. *He* had not forced her to climb the trellis. *He* had not heedlessly driven her into the street without a thought for who might be there to observe. The predicament was the lady's fault. It was she who must pay. Indeed, he should be infuriated with her for threatening his good name. He wasn't the offender; he was the victim in the deplorable catastrophe.

The *ton* would whisper about him, making him out to be a rake of the first water. Trevor didn't like that. Like most young men, he'd sown his wild oats, but his antics certainly hadn't included the violation of virtuous maidens. Moreover, those days were long past. Miss Markwell's escapade made him look like a veritable rogue. Hopefully, the *ton* would believe that his cat had torn the lady's gown, and not himself. If they did so, he should emerge relatively unscathed.

Also, he should not feel guilt at refusing to participate in Lady Nay's ruse. Miss Markwell had caused him enough grief without adding to it. She must, therefore, stand up to the *ton* on her own two feet.

Apparently, she was not willing to do so. Many days passed by without Trevor's seeing the young lady and her aunt at any social activity. He'd heard snatches of gossip, however, though no one had directly consulted him, until his best friend, Holland Farwell, came to call with one specific purpose in mind.

"Trev, I wish you'd tell me the truth of what happened between you and Miss Sophie Markwell. The scandalbroth is rampant," he said over luncheon.

Trevor took his time in answering, savoring a morsel of juicy, rare beefsteak. "It's a rather delicate subject."

"Indeed." Holly raised an eyebrow. "Perhaps you don't wish me to know all the intimate details."

"Good God, there was nothing intimate about it!" He made a face of disgust. "Just what are the scandalmongers putting out?"

His friend chuckled. "They say that Miss Markwell came to your house for the sole purpose of compromising you. Actually, most versions specify *seducing* you.''

"I see.'' Trevor looked down his straight, finely chiseled nose with disdain. "Go on.''

"Your cat tore her skirt. That could have helped her in her scheme, but for some reason, Miss Markwell became frightened at what she was doing. She bolted,'' he finished.

Trevor sipped his wine. "And how reprehensible am I in this farce?''

"The busybodies consider you innocent.''

He breathed a sigh of relief, but he couldn't help feeling sorry for the hapless Miss Markwell, even though it was her burden to bear.

"As is the case in most gossip, the story is grossly deficient,'' he told his friend. "Thoughtless of her actions, Miss Markwell angrily returned Harris, who had invaded her aunt's yard. She proceeded to admonish me for allowing him to roam the neighborhood. Then Harris ripped her skirt. She panicked and recklessly fled. That's all there was to it.''

"The brainless ninnyhammer!'' Holly marveled.

"She is naive,'' Trevor agreed.

"That's hardly the word for it. Any idiot female would know better! Miss Markwell must be as moronic as she looks.''

He felt himself bristling. "I do not consider her unattractive. Nor does she want for intelligence.''

"Really, Trevor.'' Holly grinned. "She is patently plain-faced. I cannot see why you think otherwise! You've always had an eye for a beautiful gel.''

"Her figure is superb." Trevor signaled Thorpe to clear the completed main course.

His friend guffawed. "Very well! So, you might have glimpsed a nicely turned ankle. Nevertheless, you'll have to admit that her countenance is sadly lacking. And you really should re-examine your assessment of her brain."

Trevor refused to proclaim her homely. In fact, he realized that he found Miss Markwell to be generally very alluring. He didn't understand why Holly could not see her as he did, but he didn't press that issue. He would not, however, allow the challenge to Miss Markwell's intellect to go unanswered.

"In my opinion, the lady is very quick of mind. I don't know how you can consider her feebleminded when I'll wager you've never exchanged a single word with her. I have never encountered such prejudice."

"What total foolishness!" Holly retorted. "I do not need to converse with her to perceive that she is brainless! Any young, single lady who would march right into a bachelor's dwelling hasn't the sense God gave a goose. My friend, you're far off the mark on that one!"

"Anger can cause the wisest of us to ignore conventions," he insisted.

"Not scandalous doings like that! She must be . . ."

"Holly?" Trevor exploded. *"Shut up!"*

For a long moment, his friend stared aghast at him, then frowned slightly. "My God, Trev, have you developed a *tendre* for her?"

"Of course not!" he snapped.

"I have never known you to go to such lengths to defend a woman."

"I would do the same for any man *or* woman," Trevor stated. "I regard myself as an unbiased individual."

"The Lancelot of modern damsels!" Holly chortled. "Oh Lord, you cannot wiggle out of this one! You've developed a partiality. Admit it!"

"I'll do nothing of the sort. Moreover, I am fast growing weary of this line of dialogue. Cease and desist, Holly! Instead, tell me about the big house party you're planning for All Hallow's Eve."

His friend went on as if Trevor had never made the request. "I know something of Miss Markwell that might interest you."

Trevor sighed. When Holly Farwell settled himself on a topic, he clung to it as tenaciously as a dog to a bone. He might as well allow his friend to satiate his appetite for speculation.

"I believe your Miss Markwell to be the daughter of my local vicar. I recall hearing that Bess Nay is his sister."

Trevor waited, but Holly offered no further information.

"Well?" he asked at last. "What of it?"

Lord Farwell shrugged. "I am not acquainted with Miss Markwell, if that is what you're asking. I merely thought that my recollection might be of interest to you."

"Miss Markwell and her parentage make no difference to me," he said lightly, then seized on the opportunity to direct his friend to another topic, wisely dodging even the mention of the Farwell country seat. "Would you be interested in a jaunt to Tattersall's this afternoon? There is a team of horses up for sale that I'm interested in."

"Certainly. Why not?"

Happily, Holly fell to the serious eating of his dessert. The subject of Miss Sophie Markwell was not again in contention that day. She wasn't far from Trevor's thoughts, however. It seemed that he was going to be lucky enough to escape more than a fragment of scandal. Miss Markwell would bear the brunt of the event. In short, she was ruined.

He felt a spark of sorrow for her, but he warned himself to shun fanning it into a blaze. People, as evidenced even by his best friend, were all too quick to pair him up with a female, even one considered to be damaged goods. That was the great hazard for a wealthy, bachelor peer of marital age.

Still, he was intrigued by the matter. Something about Sophie Markwell made him want to toss caution to the winds and learn more about her. It was vastly unsettling, but surely he'd recover his aplomb quite soon.

Until then, he might exchange a few words with her when next he saw her. Or he might even request a dance. But that was all. He would learn enough about her to assuage his curiosity, then go back to his normal mode of conduct. And the next time Holly attempted to accuse him of a more-than-average interest in a female, he'd turn the tables and concoct a dalliance for him!

* * *

Sophie eyed her Aunt Bess with trepidation as they alighted from the carriage and joined the crowd making their way to Sefton House. It was the first time she had appeared in public since the horrible debacle at Lord Breakstone's house, and she was absolutely terrified. No word of scandal had reached her or her aunt's ears, but Lady Nay's friends had seemed rather reluctant to converse about anything except the weather. Along with that, there were fewer invitations, though the Season should be at its busiest. Therefore, they feared the worst, but they must find out for sure. The best way to do this, they decided, was to broach the lion in his den, forging into the fray by way of accepting the Sefton request, a bid that had arrived prior to the infamous event at Lord Breakstone's home.

Surreptitiously studying the crowd through her eyelashes, Sophie noted that many of the ball-goers were regarding her with more-than-normal interest. She nudged her aunt. "People are staring so."

Lady Nay pursed her lips and sighed.

"I fear we shouldn't have come," Sophie went on. "I suppose I should have given up and returned to the country."

"Do not jump to conclusions, although it does appear that Lady Hawthorne has spread her dirt," Aunt Bess replied grimly, muscles quivering along her jaw. "Why could she not have held her tongue? It would have made no difference to her."

"She probably thinks she's performing a service,"

Sophie said direly, then mimicked the lady's high, nasal voice. "Beware of becoming serious about Sophie Markwell, gentlemen! She is meant to be a playmate, not a wife!"

"Hush," gasped her relative. "Someone will hear."

"What difference does it make? I am ruined." She unhappily lowered her chin and gazed at the brick pavement all the way to the steps.

"Don't look so defeated," Lady Nay whispered as they climbed to the stoop and entered the vestibule, giving their wraps to awaiting servants. "Maybe, knowing what we do, we are imagining things."

They were not. Their host and hostess were positively frigid with them as they passed through the receiving line. There was no doubt that the Seftons wished that they had abstained from attending.

"I have ruined your reputation, too," Sophie bitterly observed, accompanying her aunt to two empty chairs beside a large potted palm.

"No, you have not!" her aunt protested. "I shall rise above it."

Lady Nay was wrong. In public, even her closest friends avoided her, though they did send veiled glances of pity. Her other acquaintances ignored her, looking past and through her as if she were a pillar of crystal.

Sophie, of course, fared no better. People did look at her, however. Older men and especially women gave her the cut direct. Younger men pointedly glanced at her and either chuckled or appeared to mutter suggestively. Young ladies tittered behind cupped hands. She wished that a great hole would open in the floor and swallow her up.

"Let us leave," she begged her aunt.

"No!" Lady Nay snapped. "I intend to make sure that they hear *our* side of the story."

"I don't even remember what it is supposed to be."

"That you were impulsive and did not understand the crime you committed. That the cat tore your skirt."

"No one will believe it." She glumly saw Lord Breakstone take a place in the next dance figure with one of the most favored young ladies on the marriage mart. "He certainly does not seem to have suffered. You were wrong to think he'd be ruined."

"Don't jump to conclusions. That gel's parents are known to be social climbers." Aunt Bess rose. "I am going to confront my friends and make sure they know our version of the story. Believe me, I shall paint Lady Hawthorne as an exaggerating, senile, old meddler."

Sophie quickly stood, catching her arm. "Oh, Aunt, you must also depict yourself as a victim. Of me! I won't have your good standing demolished, too."

"Seat yourself, gel, and do not worry. I can take care of myself."

"I intend to seek the powder room."

"Very well, but return speedily." Aunt Bess patted her cheek and strode determinedly into the crowd which lined the dance floor.

Miserable, Sophie hurried out the nearest door, pausing for breath in the cooler hall. Her cheeks were absolutely burning with mortification. Moreover, the heat spilled from her face, descending her neck to the soft skin of her bosom. Her color must be very high. That observation shamed her even further. She not only felt guilty and was guilty, she *looked* guilty, too. Highly distressed, she hastened to the powder room.

The ladies' retiring room was actually composed of a suite of three rooms: the entrance area, which contained several chairs; a second room for repose; and a third room for more intimate needs. Entering, Sophie hesitated as she heard voices from further within.

"Can you believe that she would blithely toss away her reputation in an attempt to compromise him?"

"No!" said a second voice. "Isn't it shocking? I greatly admire Lord Breakstone for refusing to rise to the bait. Entrapment is not fair."

Someone giggled. "That's probably the only way she could land a gentleman of worth. She isn't pretty at all. And they say that her father's a vicar. No money there!"

"My brother thought her attractive," claimed a third.

"No wonder! But I doubt he's referring to her visible assets!"

The youthful ladies chortled.

"Do you really suppose that she let him have his way with her?"

"Of course! That is why she went to his house. It was part of her scheme. She is a fallen woman!"

Tears stinging her eyes, Sophie fled into the hall. She knew people were talking, but actually hearing their words was more than she could bear. She would go home. No matter how much her aunt might plot and plead and attempt to make things right, she would bolt. For starters, she would collect Aunt Bess and leave this awful party, even if she had to fib to the lady and say that she had a headache.

When she returned to the ballroom, she did not readily spot Lady Nay. Quietly crossing to the two solitary chairs, she sank down, fidgety and humiliated. If her relative did not appear soon, she vowed she'd escape to the waiting carriage. Never *ever* could she remain in the vicinity of those nameless, faceless, gossiping girls.

"Miss Markwell?" intoned a pleasant baritone at her side.

Startled, she whirled. "Lord Breakstone!"

He bowed. "May I request this dance?"

"No!" she gasped. "That is . . . it would only serve to make matters worse!"

"Indeed?" He remained bending over her. "I am not so sure of that."

"If you knew what I have heard . . ."

"And what is that?" he prompted.

"Never mind." She bent her head and peered at her hands, clenching and unclenching her fingers. "Suffice it to say that any attention you show me will be interpreted in a most negative fashion."

"I wish you'd explain more fully."

"I cannot," she said adamantly. "It would be best if you'd leave me alone."

Perversely, he sat down in Aunt Bess's unoccupied

chair. "I still believe that my regard might help you in your plight."

Sophie's heart trebled its beat. Worriedly, she flicked her gaze toward the crowded dance floor. No one seemed to be staring overtly, but she felt as if thousands of eyes were boring holes through her, as if hundreds of lips whispered feverishly, and as if tens of noses were superciliously lifted in haughty, patrician sneers.

"Lord Breakstone," she hissed, "are you attempting to punish me for my past indiscretion?"

"Not at all. I only thought to oblige. Didn't your aunt suggest that we pretend an affection for each other?"

"Fustian," she muttered. "It is too late for that, and I am not sure that it was a good idea to begin with. Now, once more I apologize for the horrible incident, although I believe that the penance Society has dealt me should be satisfactory reimbursement to you. Please leave me alone."

Although she had began with a brave speech, it ended on a rather quavering tone. His nearness was not conducive to decisive finales. Indeed, she did not want the slender thread of their association to be severed, even though it must be.

The subtle scent of his spicy cologne drifted to her nostrils. The sophisticated odor seemed to underscore the very essence of the man. Lord Breakstone was polished, elegant, and poised. The scene she'd enacted at his home must have set his teeth on edge. For the life of her, she couldn't understand why he had voluntarily sought her company . . . unless it was to make sport of her!

She mentally shook her head. That couldn't be true. Belittling her would do him no good. He must remain simply an enigma.

"Will you dance with me?" he asked again, totally disregarding her plea to be left alone.

"I have never known anyone so obtusely persistent. I have said . . ."

Before she could continue, he rose and took her hand. Fearing a scene, Sophie had no choice but to stand. "But it is a waltz!"

"Haven't you received permission to dance it?"

"Yes, some time ago, but . . ."

"Excellent." He tucked her hand through his elbow and led her to the floor.

Sophie felt as if she were performing on a stage. Everyone was gaping. The sound of whispers swelled like a freshening breeze. She closed her eyes and concentrated on the strains of the orchestra to blot out the response of the assemblage.

Luckily, she was a good dancer and had no need to focus on the steps. Also, Lord Breakstone was an exceptional partner, far more skilled than the youths who usually requested her hand in dance. Swept up in the pleasure of skimming lightly across the floor, she totally forgot their audience and danced for the simple joy of the pastime itself.

She smiled brilliantly up at Lord Breakstone.

He grinned in return. "You are an extremely talented dancer, Miss Markwell."

"As are you, my lord."

"And to think that you tried to turn me down!" Looking well pleased with himself, he suddenly whirled her in the opposite direction.

"Ha!" Sophie laughed, faultlessly following him. "Did you imagine to throw me off stride?"

"Hm, I have found it impossible. You are too accomplished for me."

Entirely too soon, the music ceased. Abruptly self-conscious of their light embrace, Sophie dropped her hands to her sides. Her happiness faded as reality returned. Most of the guests at the ball were gawking brazenly at her . . . and at him, of course, but that did not count. She felt the now-familiar heat arise in her face, neck, and bosom.

"Steady, Miss Markwell. No bolting." The marquess slipped her arm through his and escorted her back to her chair, where a wide-eyed Lady Nay awaited them.

"We must leave at once," Sophie directed her aunt as soon as she was within earshot.

"But . . ." the lady began hopefully.

"Immediately," she emphasized. She could not guess what the *ton* was collectively thinking, but it had to be terribly bad. She certainly would not stay to find out.

"I am going home if I have to walk every step of the way," she asserted.

"Walking will not be necessary, Miss Markwell. You may avail yourself of my coach," Lord Breakstone volunteered.

"We have our own conveyance," Lady Nay was quick to say, hastening to her feet. "We definitely will not invoke any more gossip by riding in yours, my lord, but we thank you just the same.''

"Yes, I suppose it would be scandalous. I didn't think of that. But I will escort you out." He offered his arm to the elder lady and ushered her from the room.

Sophie trailed them, acutely conscious of the gazes that followed their exit. She was not surprised when the voices increased to a consummate din after they'd left the room. If nothing else, the ball had made one thing painfully clear. Even if Aunt Bess had put her scheme into action, the result would have been the same. Lord Breakstone's regard only served to draw more attention to her. No claim of engagement would have fooled those people. They were not stupid! The *ton* had only to look at her face to realize that the handsome marquess would never choose her as his wife.

Holding her back ramrod straight and her chin aloft, she glided down the stairway to the entrance hall, her gaze fixed on Lord Breakstone's broad shoulders. She still did not understand his true motivation in asking her to waltz. Maybe he really did wish to help. But it was too late. It had been too late for her at the moment she first set foot in his house. Like a great army marching forward and devastating everything in its path, her foolish actions that fateful day had multiplied, each one on top of the other, until there was no relief.

Sophie did not wait for Lord Breakstone to assist her with her cloak. While he politely aided Lady Nay, she slung it over her shoulders and yanked its ties closed. She didn't even care if she tore them. In Fenster Grange, she'd have no use for formal attire. And she'd never again wear ballroom attire in London!

Lord Breakstone continued to do the pretty and ushered the ladies to their carriage. Sophie paid no heed to his and her aunt's chattering, for every time she looked at him, she grew more overset.

He seated her aunt and turned. "Miss Markwell, may I again say how much I enjoyed our dance?"

"You need not speak falsehoods," she told him.

"I do not! I did delight in . . ."

Sophie scrambled into the carriage without his assistance and nearly fell onto the squabs.

"Well, good evening to you, too, Miss Markwell," he said cynically.

When the coach began to move, Aunt Bess favored her with an arched eyebrow. "Just what was that all about? You seemed to enjoy your waltz with Lord Breakstone. What has caused this emotional turn-around?"

Sophie shrugged. "There is no future for me in London. This evening has admirably demonstrated that fact. Tomorrow, I shall leave for home."

"Oh, dear, you must postpone that, my darling," her aunt professed. "Tomorrow afternoon, you'll be driving in the park with Lord Breakstone."

"What?" Sophie screeched.

Lady Nay patiently repeated.

"I will not!" she denounced.

Her aunt moaned. "My reputation will be ruined

by falsehood. Sophie, you must go. I told him you would!''

Reputations! That's what Aunt Bess and Lord Breakstone had been chatting about! They'd been contriving a scheme. She seethed inwardly. ''Very well, Aunt Bess. I shall do so, because you wish it. But that is *all* I will do. The following day, I will leave for Fenster Grange, and nothing will stop me. Not even your reputation!''

''Thank you.'' Pleased, her aunt leaned back comfortably, and did not utter another word all the way home.

Lord Farwell was waiting for him when Trevor returned to the ball. The marquess wasn't surprised. When he'd been waltzing with Miss Markwell, he'd spied his friend on the sidelines, grinning like a Cheshire cat.

''What a charming couple you made.'' Holly grinned. ''Miss Markwell's appearance is greatly improved on the dance floor.''

''Oh?'' he replied noncommittally.

''She is obviously most talented.'' His friend inclined his head toward a group of babbling young ladies. ''You definitely set them a-stir.''

Trevor shrugged. ''They matter little to me.''

''You don't wish to dance?''

''No, I intend to leave very soon for White's.''

Holly laughed. ''All else pales when compared with the enchantment of Miss Markwell?''

Trevor glared at him. ''Once and for all, my friend,

Miss Markwell is merely the principle of the matter. I detest gossip. I wish to combat it whenever I encounter that green social demon. I singled out Miss Markwell in order to assist her in her struggle with such negative public opinion."

He ceased his hilarity, but it was easy to see that mirth lurked close to the surface.

"Now I'll be on my way to White's. Do you want to go along?"

Holly nodded assent. "I've had my quotient of giggling girls for one evening."

They took leave of their host and hostess and left the ballroom, much to the obvious chagrin of many eligible beauties.

"Y'know, Trev?" the viscount mused as they clopped along the London street in the Breakstone carriage. "You thought you were easing the gossip about Miss Markwell?"

He nodded.

"I believe you may have made it worse. By acknowledging her in public, and by dancing with her, you've left yourself wide open for speculation as to the extent of your interest."

"Nonsense!" Trevor scoffed, but he silently considered his friend's words. He'd been fully aware that he was taking a chance. He knew he'd be taking one tomorrow when he drove with her in the park. But Miss Markwell's reputation couldn't be damaged more darkly than it already was, and . . . and there was his rampant curiosity to be appeased.

"Can't we speak of anything other than the lady?" he begged. "Let us change the subject. For instance, you still haven't told me any details of the grand All Hallow's house party you are planning. I am not a great proponent of All Hallow's antics, but I expect that any festivity you offer will be vastly amusing.''

''That is what worries my Aunt Helen, who will act as my hostess!'' Holly chuckled. ''By the way, Trev, do bring that ugly cat of yours. All Hallow's would not be the same without a black cat in attendance. Perhaps we can use him as a piece in a tableau.''

Trevor nodded, though he doubted that Harris would be cooperative in any dramatic endeavor, unless he created his own event. Harris took a dim view of doing anything that was not his idea in the first place. As an actor in a farce, he would probably wreak havoc. But the marquess did not inform his friend of that fact. He wanted his cat to be welcome. If he were forced to leave Harris at home, he'd be . . . well, he'd be lonesome without him!

Sophie glanced into the hall mirror and was horrified by what she saw. When dressing for her outing with Lord Breakstone, she'd looked so pale that she had dipped into Aunt Bess's rouge pot in order to enhance her face. Then, in Lord Breakstone's presence, her natural color had added to it until her cheeks fairly flamed. And there was nothing she could do about it now. The marquess was waiting impatiently, staring at the ceiling and tapping his toe.

''I suppose I am ready,'' she muttered, turning.

He focused on her, flicking his gaze from her head

to her feet and back to her face. "Good God, girl, have you been at the paint pot?"

"I do not know what you are talking about," she said archly, "and I am not a *girl*. I have long since graduated from the schoolroom."

He grinned, nodding. "Very well, Miss Markwell, I shall remember that."

She pulled on her gloves, wishing she could dash upstairs and wash her face, but it was too late now. She was captured. Besides, he would no doubt laugh and laugh if she carried out her want.

Lady Nay, accompanied by her abigail, who also served Sophie, appeared from the nether regions of the house. "I see you are ready to go. My, but you make a handsome couple."

Sophie wished she could reply with something nasty, but she couldn't bring herself to hurt her sweet Aunt Bess.

"Kelly will be acting as chaperon," her aunt proclaimed.

The maid bobbed a curtsy to the marquess.

"Then let us be on our way," Lord Breakstone suggested.

"Yes. Do have a good time." Lady Nay frowned slightly. "Sophie, are you feeling well? Your color is so high."

"I am fine ... with the exception, of course, of being forced to participate in this charade." She lifted a wary eyebrow. "I cannot help thinking that no good will result from this business."

"Nothing can possibly go wrong." Her aunt made a shooing motion. "Go along, now."

Sophie forced herself to slip her hand through Lord Breakstone's proffered arm. Her heart seemed to somersault. She bit her lip. She must overcome this skittishness when she was in his company. But then, she really needn't worry. She probably would never ever see him again after today.

A stab of pain pierced through her breast as she thought of that. *Stop it,* she told herself sternly. She must not allow him to affect her so.

They left the house and strolled to the awaiting carriage. Attention captured by a movement in the corner of the seat, she stared into the flat, broad face of Lord Breakstone's ugly tomcat. "You are bringing that devilish beast?" she cried.

"Poor Harris!" the marquess said affectionately. "You would like him if you got to know him."

"I doubt it." Shooing the cat aside, Sophie settled herself in the forward-facing seat. Kelly sat opposite, with Lord Breakstone's cat crowding her into a corner when he decided to ride in the center of the squabs. Lord Breakstone lowered himself to the seat next to Sophie. They had scarcely traveled a block when he ordered a halt.

"Girl," he told Kelly, "seat yourself on the box with the driver. I cannot abide your staring at me as if I were a tricky culprit who is up to no good."

Shrinking, the maid swiftly obeyed.

"There," said Lord Breakstone. "I am much more comfortable. Are you not more at ease, also, Miss Markwell?"

"Not necessarily." She glanced at him sideways

through her lashes. "Are you certain that this is proper?"

"It is an open carriage. What sort of mischief could we enact?"

Sophie sniffed. "You cannot blame me for being wary. Perhaps you should sit facing me."

"For God's Sake madam, I will not do that! You are well-chaperoned. You have your maid and . . ." He grinned wickedly. ". . . you have Harris."

"Harris is the transgressor who caused this tangle. Do not speak to me of cats!"

"Now, now, Miss Markwell, you know you love felines." He chuckled. "How is the mother-to-be? I must make her acquaintance. Perhaps you should have brought her, to keep company with Harris."

She eyed his tomcat, who peered back at her with impenetrable, yellow eyes. The feline wore a red-velvet collar and leash. Such luxury in combination with his scrawny body was ludicrous. Gad, he was ugly! He certainly did not look like a suitable pet for the wealthy, sophisticated marquess. Mirth welled up inside her. She couldn't help laughing.

"You find something amusing?" the marquess queried.

"Where did you get that ill-favored cat?" she marveled.

"He adopted me one night, during a fearsome storm."

"Amazing." She shook her head slowly.

"Why is that so astonishing?" He leaned forward, picked up Harris, and settled him in his lap.

"Gentlemen usually do not like cats. They consider them effeminate."

"I know." He languidly stroked Harris's unkempt coat. "I wonder why?"

Sophie shrugged. "I could not hazard a guess, but somehow the beasts seem to pose a threat to a gentleman's manliness. I am surprised that you dare to appear publicly with your cat."

He laughed. "I have no fears about my masculinity, Miss Markwell."

Her heart fluttered. No, he should have no worries on that score. His virility was potently obvious.

She studied her hands, cheeks burning. No doubt her face was flaming an embarrassing scarlet. To Hades with the rouge!

Harris stretched and yawned, then laid out as flat and limp as a rag, closing his eyes. Lord Breakstone shook his head. "I brought him along to see the sights, and all he wishes to do is sleep."

"I am certain he's well-aware of all that goes on, if he's anything like Lady Jane." She smiled. "My cat may seem to be slumbering deeply, but if someone enters the room, she becomes instantly alert."

"A keen sense of hearing," the marquess presumed.

"Yes." Sophie wiggled her fingers toward Lord Harris, who immediately opened his eyes.

They laughed.

"I am sorry, Lord Harris, for disturbing your sleep," Sophie said.

"I thought we might leave the carriage and walk

him for a bit when we reach the park," Lord Breakstone proposed, "if you are agreeable."

"I would welcome the exercise," she concurred. "I have far too little of it in London. At home, I was accustomed to walking frequently."

"Where is your home?" he asked.

"In Fenster Grange. I doubt you've ever heard of it."

"To the contrary. I have a friend who lives there . . . Holland Farwell. Are you acquainted with him?"

"Not really. The Farwell family has seldom been in residence," she said with a slight tone of distaste. "Absentee landlords."

Lord Breakstone inclined his chin toward her. "You disapprove?"

Sophie lifted a shoulder. "Responsible people know full well what is happening on their holdings. In the case of Lord Farwell, his steward is treating the tenants very harshly."

The marquess grinned, dimples deepening. "Shall I tell Holly that he is capricious?"

A horrible vision flashed through her mind. "Oh, pray do not! My father is the vicar, and Lord Farwell owns the living. I shouldn't have spoken as I did."

"That may be," he said seriously, "but if the steward is victimizing the tenants, he is probably cheating Holly, too."

"Please do not tattle!" she begged. "I am in enough trouble. If Papa should lose his living, I shudder to think of what would become of us. We scarcely keep the wolf from the door as it is."

"Then Holly should increase his stipend."

"Dear heavens above!" she moaned. "You are getting me into grave trouble, Lord Breakstone."

He regarded her soberly. "I wouldn't dream of doing such a thing, Miss Markwell."

"I wish I were six feet under!"

"No, you don't. Then you would be unable to stir up mischief."

Sophie refused to rise to his bait, lowering her gaze and studying her hands. She remained demurely positioned as they entered the park and joined the dense line of open carriages. Though she kept her head bowed, she could feel the multitude of stares upon her.

"This is horrible," she murmured. "I can't see how Aunt thought that this masquerade would be of any benefit whatsoever."

"I, also, thought a show of friendship might silence the gossipmongers." Lord Breakstone shifted the tomcat on his lap in order to cross his legs. "Contrary to the belief of many, gentlemen are concerned with their reputations, too. I don't want people to think that I tore a woman's clothes. Nor do I wish to receive the name of harboring lightskirts in my house."

"*Lightskirts,*" she repeated, gaping at him. "You consider me a *lightskirt.*"

"I didn't say that." He tipped his hat to a barouche full of elderly ladies who nodded in return, then fell to chattering.

"I am not a lightskirt!"

He grinned. "My, but your claws are showing. Do be cheerful. Remember? We don't want to start any additional scandal by enacting a scene. Smile!"

As she looked up at him, the negative emotions she'd been grooming fled. Good heavens, he was handsome! Slightly breathless, heart thumping, she smiled shyly.

"That's better." He grinned, providing her a beautiful view of deep dimples. Seizing her hand, he tucked it through his elbow.

Taking his arm while walking was far different from this. This was a true embrace. It drew her body into close contact with his, nearly reducing her into a puddle. He continued to gaze down at her and she, up at him, until she felt lost in the blue depths of his eyes, as if she were a sinking ship floundering in the sea. Play-acting, as Aunt had suggested, was far from her mind. This was real, and abruptly she knew she was falling in love with this man, in spite of all difficulties.

After a long moment, he cleared his throat stiffly. "Let us walk now."

Trevor felt as if the sky had fallen onto his head. To look at him in such a fashion, Miss Sophie Markwell must be a consummate actress, worthy of treading the boards with the cream of Drury Lane. There'd been pure adoration in her soft, expressive eyes. Coming on the heels of her sometimes caustic remarks, the gaze had totally knocked him off stride. Just which of the several personalities was the real Sophie Markwell? What a mystery lady she was! He was fascinated.

Wanting to hold her, he lifted her from the carriage instead of assisting her to step down. When he set her on the ground, he allowed his hands to remain at her waist. Her eyes widened.

"Lord . . . Breakstone?"

He fully snapped from his trance and dropped his hands. "I'm sorry. I was woolgathering."

It was a strange time to daydream, but she did not question it. He was glad, for he didn't have the slightest idea how he would defend himself. Turning, he reached inside the carriage to pick up Lord Harris.

"I hope you don't mind if we take Harris along on our stroll."

She lifted a charming eyebrow. "I should wish I'd never laid eyes on that beast," she said dryly.

"But you don't?" he asked.

"I haven't made up my mind."

His dimples deepened. "I had hoped that you'd hold the leash."

She laughed. "Hypocrite! I might have known that you would attempt such a ploy."

"But you will go along with it?"

"Very well." She took the leash. "Come along, Harris."

But the cat had ideas of his own. He plopped down on his haunches, his head and neck pulled forward by the taunt lead. He closed his eyes.

"He isn't interested in walking." Miss Markwell stepped toward the animal, allowing him some slack.

Harris blinked.

"He's lazy." Trevor bent to pick him up.

The cat suddenly sprang to action. With a loud hiss, he swatted his paw at Trevor and leapt sideways.

Before anyone could react, he yanked the leash from Miss Markwell's hand and dashed away.

"It's a squirrel!" the lady exclaimed.

The rodent darted up a tree with the cat in hot pursuit, the leash swarping wildly to and fro.

"He'll snag the end on a branch and hang himself!" she wailed. "He'll kill himself!"

Before Trevor could run to the rescue, she rushed to the foot of the tree and began to climb, treating him to a delicious view of trim ankles. Frozen, he caught his breath as she further favored him with a display of shapely calves. He didn't stop to think that others might be taking in the sight as well until he heard a low, appreciative whistle. He whirled to see Holly, sitting on his horse and boldly staring. Reality struck. He sprinted to the tree.

"Miss Markwell! For God's sake, come down from there!"

"I almost have him!" was the reply.

"Miss Markwell!" He began to climb after her, his boots slippery on the bark.

She snagged the leash. "I've got him!"

Those were the last words before disaster. Miss Markwell tugged on the leash and dislodged Harris, who tumbled down upon her. Even the light force of the cat was enough to upset her balance. She fell backward onto Trevor. Down they went, with Trevor landing flat on his back, Miss Markwell and Harris upon him. Sometime in the midst of the performance was a horrible ripping noise. The next sound Trevor heard was raucous laughter.

"Oh, my goodness!" shrieked Miss Markwell, looking down into his face. "My gown!"

He gaped at the torn sleeve and shoulder hem.

"Oh, my!" Face scarlet, she jumped to her feet, holding Harris up to hide her bare skin.

Trevor managed to stand. "Are you all right?"

"No!" she wrenched out. "My dress!"

Holly maneuvered his horse between the scene and the gathering crowd of onlookers on the carriage way. "Your coat, Trev!" he urged.

"What?"

"Your coat! Put your coat around her!"

Trevor snapped into action. Slipping hurriedly out of the garment, he draped it across her shoulders and took Harris from her arms.

Thrusting the cat into his hands, Miss Markwell tightly clasped the coat, drawing it snugly around her. "I cannot believe this! Every time I am around that cat, disaster strikes!"

Harris purred.

"Please accept my humblest apologies," Trevor began. "It was the . . ."

"Be still!" she growled. "Take me home at once! To my aunt's house that is. I shall *really* be going home tomorrow. To Fenster Grange!"

Trevor was miserable. This time, the devastation was his fault. If he had not taken her driving . . . if he hadn't taken Harris driving . . . Dash it all! He hadn't caused Miss Markwell to climb the tree after Harris. That she came to grief was, once more, her fault. But he didn't tell her that. She had meant well.

She'd thought that Harris was in danger and had sprung to help him. He offered his arm.

"I shall take you home, Miss Markwell. To your aunt's, that is."

She looked into his eyes, that searching look that had earlier mesmerized him. He could see the pique drain from her face and the corners of her mouth begin to twitch. She finally smiled.

"Lord Breakstone, I believe it might be more prudent if I used both of my hands to clutch your coat." She sniffed its lapel in a gesture that surprised him. "Your cologne is marvelous."

He suddenly remembered Holly, sitting there, all ears, and waiting to tease him unmercifully. "Thank you, Miss Markwell. Shall we go now?"

They strolled toward the carriage as if nothing had happened in spite of the small, whispering knot of people who had gathered to watch. The lady studiously ignored them, entering the coach and sitting primly and cooly as if butter wouldn't melt in her mouth. Trevor turned to Holly.

"I appreciate your assistance, my friend, but I'm hoping you'll hold your tongue about it."

The viscount grinned and winked, giving Trevor no clue as to what he would do.

Trevor placed Harris on the seat and climbed in. "Lady Nay's," he told the coachman, then glanced at Miss Markwell. "I am truly sorry that the afternoon was spoilt."

She shrugged. "What could be expected?"

Harris licked his paws and looked pleased with himself. Rising, he stretched and then jumped across the chasm between seats and into Miss Markwell's lap. Yawning, he snuggled down.

She eyed him helplessly. "Goodness gracious. I cannot fathom how such a little animal could have caused such a big predicament. Ah well, all will soon be past."

For the rest of the way home, Trevor attempted to make conversation with her, but she would not be drawn out. She merely gazed at the passing scenery and absently stroked Lord Harris. When he deposited her in Lady Nay's entrance hall, she politely bid him farewell and remarked that she would be leaving in the morning for the country.

As he walked away, Trevor, to his horror, realized that he didn't want her to leave. Not at all.

III

Fall 1816

Sophie had not realized that she would dislike leaving London so very much, not particularly for the parties, shopping, and cultural events, but because of the marquess. Something indefinable had passed between them during those last days in town. She wondered if he'd noticed it, too, and decided that he probably had not. In those few, brief moments that their gazes had locked, she had learned, without a doubt, that she was in love with him. But of course, Lord Breakstone could never love her in return.

Even in the beginning of the Season when anything seemed possible, Sophie had always been realistic in her marital outlook. She'd never hoped for more than a man of lower rank but good family, who was well-enough-to-do, and who would be a kind and considerate husband. She wasn't pretty enough and her family wasn't wealthy enough for her to have set her sights higher. Lord Breakstone was a very big catch in a small social pond. Everything about him was simply perfect. He would go to a young lady of great beauty whose family ranked high in wealth and nobility. For her, he was only a dream.

But he was definitely a fantasy who was very hard to erase from her mind. In the first few weeks at home in Fenster Grange, Sophie mourned for him as she would a lost lover. Even now, as she assisted her mother in planning for the Harvest Festival on All Hallow's Eve, her mind wandered to thoughts of him. It was a habit that was altogether oversetting.

"Sophie," Mrs. Markwell said in a vigorous voice, "you are woolgathering again."

She startled. "Oh, Mama, I am sorry. I don't know what has come over me of late."

The elder woman laughed softly. "If I didn't know the truth, I'd think your tendency toward oblivion was caused by a gentleman."

Sophie didn't tell her that she was right, that only a moment ago she was daydreaming of Lord Breakstone. She had told them as little as possible about the marquess. They wouldn't have laughed or made sport if she'd told them she loved him, for they were a caring and thoughtful family; but they would have known that such a match existed only in fairy tales. Their sympathy would have been harder to bear than their teasing.

"There was not a particular gentleman whom you

hated leaving, was there?'' Mrs. Markwell asked. ''You have been awfully moody, Sophie.''

''I left no one whom I could have hoped to marry,'' she replied evasively. ''I was merely pondering how disappointing I must be to you and Papa . . . for my failure in London.'' That was the truth, although not the complete reality, for she'd also been fantasizing about Lord Breakstone.

''You could never be a disappointment!'' her mother cried. ''You have always been the sweetest of daughters, my dear.''

''But not the brightest.'' She smiled wistfully. ''If I had heeded Papa's teachings, I wouldn't have stormed into Lord Breakstone's house like a total fool.''

''That is past now. Let us think of the future instead.''

''There are still some parishioners who look upon me with suspicion.'' She shook her head. ''I wonder how word of my misdeeds reached Fenster Grange.''

''Bad news gallops, while good news walks,'' Mrs. Markwell said dryly. ''But everyone in the area, even those who seem to mistrust you, know that you were truly innocent in the matter.''

''I pray that is so.'' Sophie sighed. ''I have caused you and Papa great heartache.''

''Only because you, yourself, are distressed.''

''You probably thought you'd be rid of me. Now you not only have my returning mouth to feed, but you have Lady Jane and six kittens to nourish,'' she moaned.

Mrs. Markwell chortled. ''Those are the least of my

worries. Taking center stage in my mind is this Harvest Festival.''

"Do you mean the All Hallow's Eve celebration?" Sophie teased, casting off her gloom.

They exchanged smiles. Reverend Markwell was a well known opponent of All Hallow's, considering it a pagan rite which had no place in the lives of modern, God-fearing people. He had not been able to sway his flock to his point of view, however. The parishioners *would* have their fete! So, a compromise was reached, allowing the neighborhood Harvest Festival, in the form of a fair, to be held on October 31, with the proceeds of the booths going to the church. Thus, the vicar celebrated the harvest and the funds swelling the church's budget, while his congregation enjoyed All Hallow's.

"As usual, I'm to bake pies," Sophie's mother informed her, "and this year the committee wants even more."

"I am not surprised," Sophie said. "Your apple pies are greatly renowned."

Mrs. Markwell could scarcely disguise the pride on her face. "Will you help me? You make them just as well as I."

"I cannot match your skill!" she protested. "But yes, you may depend upon me."

"Good! I thought we'd drive out to Farmer Murchison's this afternoon to obtain the fruit."

Sophie nodded. "I'll also ask the Murchisons if they need any cats."

For some time, the kittens had been ready to leave their mother, but Sophie hadn't had the heart to separate them, until her patient father had mentioned it last night at dinner. Several years ago, the Murchisons had taken two kittens from Lady Jane's litter, so they might not need any more mousers, but it was worth a try. Mrs. Murchison adored cats, and though the felines were supposed to catch mice for their supper, she often supplemented the meal with table scraps. Knowing the kittens would have a good home on that farm, Sophie loaded Lady Jane and her brood into a box and set it in the cart as she and her mother prepared to leave. The very sight of the babies would sorely tempt the farmer's wife.

With her mother beside her, Sophie took the reins and drove through the village. It was a beautiful fall day, the sun shining brightly, creating a red-and-gold aura under the changing trees. The air was sweet with the fresh scent of rich earth and dry leaves.

"Ah, on days like this, it is good to be alive!" Mrs. Markwell declared, breathing deeply of the fresh air.

Sophie agreed. She could almost forget Lord Breakstone in this glorious weather. Almost . . . but not quite.

As they reached the crossroads to turn toward the Murchison farm, a large, crested traveling coach thundered past them at a high rate of speed.

"Such driving!" Sophie criticized. "Where on earth could they be going in such a hurry?"

"To Farwell Hall, I imagine," her mother suggested. "I was speaking with the housekeeper, just the other day. Lord Farwell apparently is hosting a large house party for All Hallow's."

Sophie's heart leapt to her throat. Lord Farwell was

Lord Breakstone's best friend. The marquess would surely attend.

"It will be strange to have a Farwell in residence," Mrs. Markwell mused. "I wonder if he will bring his guests to our humble festival."

"Probably not," Sophie guessed. "It wouldn't be fine enough for him."

"No?" Her mother lifted an eyebrow. "How do you know? Did you become acquainted with Lord Farwell in London?"

"Barely." She winced inwardly as she remembered the viscount, sitting on his horse and witnessing her final disgrace. At least he had tried to help. If he hadn't made himself a living screen, the scene would have been far worse.

"It would be a blessing if he spent more time at Farwell Hall," mused her mother. "Perhaps this party is a sign of better stewardship to come. I certainly hope it is. Some of those tenant houses aren't fit for beasts!"

Sophie wondered if Lord Breakstone had informed his friend of the state of affairs at his estate and, if so, what Lord Farwell would do about the matter. She didn't consider it long, however. The prospect of Lord Breakstone being nearby claimed her thoughts.

Would she see him? *No,* she sternly told herself. Lord Breakstone would never come calling on a lowly vicar's daughter, and she certainly would not be invited to Farwell Hall. On their brief visits, the family had always held themselves aloof from local affairs. They seldom even went to church. No, her only chance would be if Lord Farwell brought his guests to the festival to view what they'd term *quaint villagers*. If he did that, Lord Breakstone would probably appear with a beautiful, eligible young lady on his arm. And he wouldn't notice Sophie at all.

Her mother cut through her reverie. "You're awfully quiet again, Sophie. Is it because I made mention of Lord Farwell?"

Her cheeks burned. She was glad she was attired in her cloak so that it would hide the flush which spread down her neck to suffuse her bosom.

"Have you a *tendre* for Lord Farwell?" Mrs. Markwell quizzed.

Sophie shook her head. "No."

"A viscount would be a great catch for a vicar's daughter. Although it would be a lengthy step upward on the social ladder, it wouldn't be an unheard-of match. There is nothing wrong in reaching high."

"I suppose not," she replied noncommittally.

"Where did you meet the young man?"

"In the park. Mama, do not attempt to read anything into the situation."

Mrs. Markwell laughed lightly. "One never knows."

Sophie had not told them of her awful adventure in the park. One incident had been enough to shock them out of their wits. A second disaster would have caused them to faint dead away.

"What a coupe it would be if my girl wed a viscount!" her mother marveled. "As a vicar's wife, I must be unassuming, but surely I would be pardoned if I were a little bit smug."

"Mama, leave off," she begged. "I had only a fleeting introduction to Lord Farwell. I doubt that he even remembers it.''

"One never knows," her mother repeated.

Sophie wondered how her parent would react if she revealed her hopeless love for a marquess. That would definitely bowl her over. Why, Lord Breakstone was a member of the upper echelon of the upper echelon!

She remembered how his marvelous eyes had searched hers. Her heart pounded rapidly. Tears prickled her eyes.

"Sophie?" her mother asked quietly. "I know that something is wrong, something more than the unfortunate episode at Lord Breakstone's residence. Do you wish to tell me? Sometimes it helps to share."

She had kept her feelings bottled for far too long. Seeing through a veil of tears, she pulled the horse off the road and under a huge oak tree. Her story, and the accompanying tears, came spilling forth.

"Mama, I knew all along that it was preposterous. I am too plain-faced; I have no large dowry! But I couldn't help it. I fell in love with him," she finished, sobbing.

"Now, now," her mother crooned, taking her in her arms and comforting her like a child. "It's all right."

"Is it?" she wailed. "How can I ever forget him?"

"Time heals all wounds, my darling. Someday, when you are happy with a fine husband and children, you will look back and wonder what you ever saw in Lord Breakstone." She took a handkerchief and wiped Sophie's eyes and cheeks. "It hurts terribly now, but relief will come."

Snuffling, Sophie tried to regain control of her emotions. "Mama, may I stay home from the Harvest Festival? If Lord Farwell did bring his guests and I saw Lord Breakstone . . . Please allow me the respite. If I came face-to-face with the marquess, I just know that I'd go completely to pieces!"

"Very well, if that is what you wish," Mrs. Markwell stated, giving her a final hug. "You needn't attend."

"What shall I tell Papa?"

"Leave your father to me." She nodded confidently. "I shall tell him all he needs to know."

"I don't want the rest of the family to know about Lord Breakstone!" she beseeched.

"I'll admit I'm surprised that you didn't tell your sister Jane. The two of you are very close."

Sophie smiled sadly. "I was too embarrassed. But . . . but I'm glad I told you. It does help to have another person know."

"I'm glad." She tucked a loose strand of silky hair back under her daughter's bonnet. "Maybe the wound will heal more quickly now that you know you may depend on my sympathy."

Sophie doubted that the pain of loving Lord Breakstone would ever entirely leave her, but she hoped that her mother was right. Neither could she imagine ever loving another man. In fact, if she carried through with her agenda, she would never wed.

Wishing to spend the holidays with her family, she planned to wait until January to apply for positions of governess or companion. She had not yet told her parents of her outline for the future. Now, starting the horse down the road, she revealed her idea to her mother.

"Aren't you being a bit hasty?" Mrs. Markwell inquired.

"I don't think so." She shook her head. "There is no future for me here. And the family could certainly use my wage. A vocation seems like a reasonable thing to pursue."

"You absolutely must discuss this course with your father before proceeding."

"I shall, but I have lots of time before I act." She tipped the whip, setting the horse into a jog. "Of the two occupations, I believe I would enjoy working with children the most. I think I'd be good at it."

Her mother slowly shook her head. "It would be far better if they were your own."

"Yes, of course! But that is out of the question."

Sophie slowed the horse to turn into the Murchison lane, then set him trotting again. They pulled up in the barnyard with a jaunty halt as Murchisons seemed to appear from all directions. As Sophie had wished, Mrs. Murchison fell in love with two of Lady Jane's fluffy offspring and took them into the dairy. Then, Mr. Murchison and his eldest son, Carl, brought forth a bushel basket of bright red apples and, also, a lovely smoked ham as a harvest gift to the vicar's family.

Carl paused by Sophie's side of the cart. "You'll be going to the festival, I guess?"

"No one misses the Harvest Festival!" she said brightly, neither saying yea or nay. The Murchison son had been sweet on her for ages, despite her lack of encouragement. She hoped he would not be too greatly disappointed when she failed to appear.

"This year, I know I'll win a prize in the ball-throwing booth," he said confidently. "You may select it and keep it always."

She lowered her gaze. "You are too kind."

"Never!" he exclaimed. "I could never be as kind as you deserve, Miss Sophie. And I'm glad you stood your ground to a cheeky nob! But I'm happier still that you came home. I don't mean to be disrespectful of Our Lord, but you brighten the whole church when you're there!"

"What a charming thing to say, sir." She smiled. "Now we must be on our way."

"I've a bit of money saved," he disclosed. "I'm sure going to buy one of your pies!"

"The church will be grateful." She took up the reins. "Farewell, Mr. Murchison."

He trotted a short way beside the cart. "I'll see you soon, Miss Sophie!" he called, dropping back as she urged the horse to a speedier gait. "Don't forget to watch me at the ball-throwing booth!"

Sophie waved.

"You've certainly made a conquest there," her mother remarked. "The Murchisons are quite well-to-do, genteel people. One could do worse than to marry among them."

"No," Sophie said firmly. "I shall not solicit the regard of Carl Murchison."

"I don't think you need to actively invoke it." She laughed lightly. "It appears that you've already stolen the young man's heart."

"I hope not." She frowned. "I do not wish him to be hurt, for I could never wed him, Mama. Not when my heart is possessed by another."

"I wish you could envision the practicality . . ."

"I do." Sophie nodded curtly. "I shall be a governess or a companion."

They drove the rest of the way in silence.

In the late afternoon sunshine, the village of Fenster Grange looked as if it were bathed in gold when Trevor rode toward it. It was a picturesque hamlet of Tudor half-timbered, thatch-roofed dwellings; a verdant green commons, and bright cottage gardens. The marquess, however, focused his eyes on the little stone church and its graveyard. Nearby would be the vicarage, somewhere in that clump of brilliant trees. Was she even now within?

Since Sophie Markwell had left London, Trevor had to admit that the days had lost much of their luster. He'd thought that he'd quickly forget her, but that hadn't happened. If anything, he thought of her more every day. Under any circumstances, he would have come to his friend's house party, but the possibility of seeing Miss Markwell had added a special excitement to the excursion.

Through wily questioning, he discovered that Holly had not invited the lady to his house party. Her name had been even more darkened by the piece of nonsense in the park. To add her to the guest list would have been an insult to many illustrious members of the *ton* who would be in attendance. It aggravated

Trevor, but there was nothing he could do about it. Perhaps he would chance upon her while out riding or visiting the village. Or he might attend church. She surely would be there. But he was reticent about actually calling on her. He wasn't certain what sort of welcome he would receive.

Trevor was merely curious to find out how she had fared when she'd told her parents of her disasters. There was nothing more, of course. He simply needed assurance that she had risen above her difficulties. After all, he was involved. He must assuage his conscience.

He reached the lane to Farwell Hall before he went through the town. Turning, he passed through an arch which was flanked by two immense stone griffins. His traveling coach, bearing his valet and clothing, followed behind.

It was not a long way from the gates to the house. As Trevor pulled up in front, Holly hurried out, waving. The marquess slipped down from his horse and tossed the reins to an awaiting stable lad.

"Greetings, Holly!" he called. "Had you given up on me?"

His friend strode up to him. "Most of the guests did arrive yesterday."

"My tardiness was unavoidable. Business, you know." He ambled back to the traveling coach and removed Harris from within.

"Well, you're here now, and that's what counts." Holly led him toward the house. "I'll wager you'd appreciate a glass of brandy to settle the dust of the road."

"That would be most welcome."

They climbed the steps and entered a large, oak-paneled hall. Lord Farwell gestured toward a door on the right.

"Most of the other guests are in the drawing room. Would you care to join them? Or we may escape to the library for a brief repast. Some of the gentlemen are there."

"The library," he chose without hesitation. "I'll greet the ladies later, after I've shed this layer of highway dust."

"Well, it doesn't bother me. You still look like you've just stepped out of a tailor's establishment." Holly led the way down the hall to the room. Several old friends rose to welcome them. Trevor gratefully accepted a glass of brandy and sat down, cradling Harris in his lap.

"That is, beyond a doubt, the ugliest cat I've ever seen," observed Lord Corville.

"He's so ugly he's fascinating," ventured Lord Kendall.

Harris did look particularly disreputable at the moment. He'd been fighting, and one of his ears was bitten. Also, he was bored, as evidenced by the drunken expression on his face.

Holly chuckled. "He's a battered old warrior, isn't he? But he's the perfect centerpiece for All Hallow's Eve. I'm glad you brought him, Trev."

Idly sipping his brandy, Trevor stroked Harris's disheveled fur. He'd long since decided not to take offense at people's comments on the cat's disreputable appearance. After all, Harris *was* ugly, but his intriguing personality made up for it.

"Never knew a man to have a cat for a pet," Corville proclaimed, drinking deeply. "They're women's toys."

Trevor tensed, wondering if the day had come, at last, when he would have to defend his manliness.

Holly stepped in to allay the comment. "If you'll carefully examine this cat, you'll see that he wouldn't complement a lady. Look at his battle scars! He's the epitome of feline masculinity."

Kendall guffawed. "He's still just a little cat."

Trevor set his drink aside.

"That's enough," Holly protested. "I don't want my party to be marred by a duel. Especially over that tomcat!"

Harris yawned and licked his lips.

"Playing with cats is effeminate," Corville went on. "You may as well admit it, Breakstone, for you know it's true."

"Maybe you'd take a different view if you had your teeth poked down your throat," Trevor retorted. "I have no need to prove my virility to you or anyone else."

"Ooh!" screeched Kendall in a high-pitched voice. "Don't sic your little pussy on us!"

Setting Harris aside, Trevor rose.

"Stop it!" Holly tried to intervene. "Gentlemen, this is uncalled for! We're trying to have a good time and celebrate All Hallow's Eve. Let's duel with spooks and skeletons, not with each other!"

"All right." Corville sat back in his chair, negligently crossed his legs, and grinned up at the marquess. "Duel with ghosts? Very good! You can spend All Hallow's in the graveyard, Breakstone. That should tell the tale of your true gender."

"Yes!" agreed Kendall. "You can take along your kitty cat for company."

"This is ridiculous," Holly objected. "He doesn't need to prove a thing! The two of you are tipsy or you wouldn't question it. Moreover, he'd miss the party."

"Then we'll make the test last only a few hours . . . say nine o'clock to midnight. How about it, Breakstone?" Corville said gleefully. "I'll even sweeten it up with a wager. Are you game?"

"This is so stupid," their host disparaged.

"I'll do it." Trevor crossed the room to the liquor cabinet to refill his glass. "I'm not afraid of haunts. There is no such thing."

"Just wait till you're in the cemetery!" Kendall laughed. "You might just change your mind!"

"Fustian," said Trevor. "You two are the ones who would be afraid or you wouldn't have come up with the test."

After that, the topic changed to other subjects of lesser daring, but Trevor's mind kept returning to the challenge. Happily, he'd never numbered ghosts among his phobias. Only storms and spiders! So, being in the graveyard offered no hazard to his equilibrium. In fact, he was glad of the dare. He'd be near the home of Sophie Markwell and could ascertain the lay of the land without anyone questioning his mission. Perhaps he'd even chance to see her.

Time passed quickly for him. After a delectable dinner, the guests prepared for a visit to the villagers' Harvest Festival. There'd be a big bonfire with food, dancing, and general revelry. Learning of that, Trevor was disappointed to be positioned in the cemetery. Miss Markwell probably would be attending the festivities. He'd miss a golden opportunity to see her.

Hopefully she would stay late, he told himself, and he could speak with her after his vigil. Or he might see her coming or going and could call to her. He'd survey the situation and post himself as close as possible to the vicarage and still stay within the guidelines of the bet.

Satisfied with this line of reasoning, he picked up his cat and grinned into his placid face. "Well, Harris, are you ready to sojourn with skeletons?"

The cat merely blinked.

"Very well, that's what we'll do." Cheerfully, he joined in other topics of male conversation.

The local cemetery lay shrouded in a swirling, gray fog. Through the vague outline of the lych-gate, one could see the ghostly forms of tall, flat headstones; narrow obelisks, and pyramidal yews. An owl hooted its long, trailing wail of woe.

The carriage drew to a halt, horses stamping restlessly, as if wary of remaining in this place of mortality for more than the briefest moment. The coachman leapt briskly down from the box. He jerked open the door and stood shifting from foot to foot, as if he, too, were impatient to hasten away.

One of the three occupants chuckled and lifted a hand of restraint. "Are you sure you want to do this, Breakstone? The graveyard looks rather formidable. Can't say that I'd blame you for conceding."

"That's right," Holly seconded. "No one'll think the less of you for it. Any sane man would be home, toasting his toes by the fireside."

"I don't know about that," Lord Corville differed. "It's too warm for a fire, and besides, I thought we were going to the village's festival."

"Who cares?" said Holly. "I'm only proffering an example."

"Even so, you should . . ." Kendall began.

"Farewell," Trevor interrupted, swooping Lord Harris from his lap to his arms. "I'll see you gentlemen later."

Corville scooted to the edge of the seat. "Why don't you cry off, Breakstone? There'll be evil things abroad this night." The marquess negligently lifted a shoulder. "The myth of ghosties and ghoulies does not frighten me. This will be the easiest challenge I've ever met."

An unseasonably warm breeze brought the scent of rich earth and moldering leaves to Trevor's nostrils. The owl trilled again and was answered by its mate. Trevor felt cool beads of perspiration form on his upper lip. Now that he was on the scene, he was not precisely frightened, but neither was he as self-assured as he'd thought he would be. But then, wouldn't most people be rather reluctant to face the lonely, eerie site?

"Skeletons will be clacking in a macabre dance," Corville warned.

"Give up on it, Breakstone!" Kendall urged, grinning. "Avoid the scent of putrefying, rotting flesh!"

"May the two of you strangle on your colorful imaginings." Trevor stepped down from the coach. "Begin counting out your coins. I'll collect shortly after midnight!"

"Milord?" The coachman stuck his finger in his stock and tugged at it. "The locals, they say that the graveyard's truly haunted."

"Isn't that always said of cemeteries?" Trevor smiled. "Thank you for the warning, but I really don't believe in that sort of thing."

"Let us go to our revels," Corville proclaimed. "This fool will not be deterred."

Kendall leaned out. "Go along, Breakstone. Remember, you must go to the very heart of the place!"

"I am aware of the details." Trevor turned and walked toward the villagers' final resting place. As he passed through the lych-gate, he heard the carriage pull away, horses' hooves grinding into a trot.

"Well, Harris," he said aloud. "Now we'll have a long, boring wait, unless we see Miss Markwell, of course. But one way or the other, you'll have some exercise. And who knows, you might even scare up a mouse or two!"

Still carrying the cat, he picked his way among the tombstones, tripping now and then on the heaving hillocks or sunken depressions of the sod. A large colony of moles was obviously at work in the cemetery, making the footing treacherous. Trevor swore lightly as his booted foot plunged into a patch of spongy soil. He'd be lucky if he didn't break his ankle, wandering around in the dark like this. He wished he'd brought a lantern, but he supposed that wouldn't have been allowed.

Immediately spotting what must have been the vicarage, he made his way toward it, but halted sufficiently far enough into the graveyard to adhere to the challenge. He sat down on a raised crypt, releasing Lord Harris. "Don't wander too far away," he admonished, "and come back when you're called."

The black feline stretched luxuriously, arched his back, then disappeared quietly into the night.

Loneliness descended like a heavy cloud upon Trevor, even though he knew that his cat was nearby. In the distance, he heard shouting and laughter and saw the flare and the shooting sparks of a huge bonfire. The residents of the hamlet had begun their evening celebration. Centuries ago, before the church made it palatable, their festival would have been a pagan ritual. Even now, deep within most souls, lay a primitive fear which caused the merrymakers to dance a bit more wildly and to behave with unaccustomed abandon. Most of the group from the manor had planned to join the townspeople in their festivities. Holly, Kendall, and Corville had probably arrived, perhaps hoping to reap the bounty of some willing, country wenches.

But Trevor's solitude was not assuaged by the relative nearness of people. Nor by the nearby house with the glowing windows, which surely must be the vicar's residence. Who else would live beside a burial ground?

He wondered if Sophie were within the home or if she had gone to the frolic. He had to see her. Here, alone in the dark, he faced the brutal truth. He needed her in his life. He was in love with her.

Though the admission should surely have made the night become brighter, it suddenly seemed much darker. The flirtatious breeze blew harder. Trevor looked up at the moon and saw it flying frantically amid threatening clouds. There was a distinct growl of thunder. His stomach cramped.

No. Not now. Not tonight!

He set his jaw. It was ridiculous, he told himself, this abominable fear of storms. It was time he came to grips with it. He stared bravely up at the whirling skies and tensed as lightning slashed a jagged path through the darkness. He gritted his teeth when thunder rolled again.

"Come now, Breakstone," he muttered aloud. "A drenching is the worst thing that will happen to you. You must defeat this phobia if you wish to act on your feelings for Sophie Markwell and ask her to be your bride."

This reasoning did not help at all. The wind began whipping in earnest. The moon totally disappeared behind angry, black clouds, relinquishing all illumination to the flashing bolts of lightning. Thunder boomed.

"Harris!" Trevor shouted, voice cracking.

There was no answering meow.

"Harris!" he called again, rising. He gazed longingly at the safe, warm vicarage, but made no move in that direction. He was still determined to win the wager and, more than that, to rid himself of this debilitating weakness. The cat's company would help.

"Harris! Dammit, come here!"

The wind snatched the hat from his head and carried it into the inky night. Droplets of rain struck his heated face. Overhead, a bough creaked and groaned.

Trevor shuddered as thunder crashed. Once more sitting down, he drew up his legs, encircled his knees with his arms, bent his head, and cringed. His heart seemed to pound like the drumming of horses' hooves at full gallop. Would this terror never end? Though it had only been minutes, it seemed like hours since the storm had begun. He bit his lip until he tasted the slightly salty, metallic flavor of blood. Rain pelted him. He began to shake uncontrollably.

How surprised Corville and Kendall would be if they knew what really scared him out of his wits, he thought grimly, teeth chattering. There were no ghosts in this graveyard. There was only the sheer terror, never outgrown, of a lonely little boy.

Lightning brilliantly bathed the cemetery in a beam bright as day. For a fleeting second, Trevor glimpsed a sight which made him question his own sanity. A misty gray apparition was weaving in and out among the tombstones and heading in his direction, its lantern nearly sweeping the ground. Trevor leapt to his feet. Good God, hadn't he enough phobias in his life? Must he add the fear of ghosts to his list?

He watched intently, actually hoping for a burst of

lightning so that he might see more clearly. When it came, he saw, with horror, the terrible form, its cloak billowing in the wind. His heart vaulted to his throat. He began to back up in retreat toward the road.

"There you are, you naughty baggage!" shrilled the wraith. "Why have you been hiding from me on such a night as this?"

Simultaneously, Trevor stumbled over a footstone and fell heavily onto his back.

"Who's there?" cried the ghost.

The marquess struggled for breath.

"Answer me!" the shade demanded and hove into view, lifting its lantern high. "Good Heavens! It's Lord Breakstone! Sir, what are you doing on Tom Moore's grave?"

As lightning flashed, Trevor gazed into a pair of unforgettable eyes. Relief flooded over him. The would-be specter wasn't a spirit at all. He grinned self-consciously.

"Sophie? What are you doing here?"

"I might ask the same. I might also ask who gave you leave to address me so informally." She bent to pick up her gray cat. "I am here because I happen to live here."

"It is a rather fitting habitat for a witch such as yourself," he observed, getting to his feet and stepping off the mound of earth that marked the remains of the villager.

"I live in the vicarage," she snapped. "I am the vicar's daughter."

"I remember. How could I forget? It's such an unsuitable role." He would have said more, but a bolt of lightning and a gigantic clap of thunder claimed his attention. He winced mightily.

She gaped. "Heavens above! Are you afraid of the storm?"

"No, I am not." He tried to muster some dignity, but another earth-shattering rumble spoiled his attempt. He trembled.

"You are!" she accused and gestured toward the house. "Well, come on! We're being drenched! There is a safe haven in the vicarage."

He gladly followed her for several paces, then reluctantly halted. "I have to find Harris!" he shouted above the storm.

"That awful cat is here?"

"You would like Harris if you got to know him." Thunder boomed, causing Trevor to flinch once more.

"I am impressed," she said. "You are terrified, yet you are thinking of your cat. That is admirable, Lord Breakstone."

"Harris!" he called, then looked beseechingly at her. "I wish you would not dwell on my opinion of storms."

"Why not? When it is so obvious . . ."

The black tomcat suddenly sprang onto a tombstone beside them and squalled, startling them both.

"Trickster." Trevor plucked him from his perch.

"Come on!" the lady urged. "I'm cold and I'm wet!"

He ran beside her, cursing himself. He had found her, only to be thoroughly unmanned by his awful phobia. No doubt Sophie Markwell was inwardly laughing so hard that her sides were paining her. He wished he had never admitted to himself that he loved her. He couldn't ask her to marry him. Who would wed a man with such an unreasonable fear?

"This way!" she directed, leading him to the back door of the residence, setting down the lantern and wrenching it open. "Oh, what a downpour!"

He followed her into the welcome sanctuary. The vicarage kitchen was warm and sweet-smelling of cinnamon and apples. Trevor took a deep breath of the marvelous aroma. He had never been inside a kitchen, but if this were typical, the rooms were wonderful places to be. He glanced around, taking in the big, flaming hearth; the long, scrubbed table; the pots and pans.

"There is nothing wrong with a kitchen on a dark and stormy night," she said rather defensively.

"No. Not at all! It's most comforting." He shivered, but this time from his wet chill and not from the tempest.

She removed her cloak and placed it on a peg by the door. "You are soaked. Let me take your coat."

He set Harris on the flagged floor and removed the garment.

She spread it across a bench near the fire. "It should dry quickly. Now perhaps you'd like some mulled wine? And a piece of apple pie?"

"I know of nothing I'd like better," he declared.

"Then sit down at the table," she ordered and stared at Harris. "You disagreeable tomcat! I suppose you must have some warm milk. And you, too," she added, nodding to Lady Jane.

Thunder clapped, but Trevor didn't startle.
Strange . . . he didn't feel so nervous when he was in
Sophie's presence. *Sophie.* How sweet her name was!
Yes, he'd continue to call her by her Christian name,
at least to himself if she remained bent on protesting
it. He grinned as lightning flashed. The storm was
almost nice. It caused things to seem very cozy. Perhaps *she* was the key to overcoming his fear. He
gradually relaxed, watching her move about the
kitchen. By Jove, he was actually *glad* it had stormed!

Sophie was so cheerful that she almost sang as she
went about preparing the repast for Lord Breakstone.
She thought of how often, in the past few days, she
had pictured him nearby at Farwell Hall. She'd been
so tempted to concoct an excuse to visit the estate in
hopes of getting a glimpse of him. Now here he was,
right in the kitchen! Thank Heavens for storms and
for whatever reason he had been in the graveyard.
Thank goodness that Lady Jane had escaped from
the house when she had gone out for wood—and
disappeared into the night. Thanks, thanks, thanks!
She served the marquess, then the cats, and sat
down at the table. "Is everything all right?"
"Delicious! Whoever made this pie is an artist."
She smiled, lowering her eyes. "I did."
"You?" he exclaimed. "You truly know how to
make something like this?"
"A vicar's daughter does not have servants to wait
on her hand and foot, my lord," she reminded, then

suddenly remembered the festival. "I made pies for the festivity. I fear these last ones won't be needed."

"This torrent is enough to drown the largest bonfire," he predicted. "I'm sure the party has ended."

"My whole family must be drenched. I daresay they've taken refuge in the nearest cottage." She eyed him curiously. "Why, may I ask, were you in the cemetery?"

"A wager." He chuckled. "I suppose I've lost it."

"The storm should have canceled it."

He shook his head. "It won't."

"But, Lord Breakstone . . ."

"Trevor," he told her.

Sophie wasn't sure that she was hearing him correctly. Had he really asked her to call him by his first name? She tilted her chin. "I beg your pardon?"

"Trevor. Won't you call me *Trevor*? After all, I do intend to call you *Sophie.*"

She flushed. "It really is not proper. *Trevor* is a nice name, however. It speaks of valor."

He laughed shortly. "Not hardly . . . You should know from what you witnessed in the graveyard."

"That you are afraid of storms? Pshaw!" She shrugged. "Everyone is afraid of one thing or the other."

He studied her intently. "You don't consider it reprehensible?"

"No." She smiled. "Why should I? It doesn't signify."

"I cannot bear spiders either!" he said in a rush.

"Neither can I!" She quivered demonstrably. "Horrid creatures! They make my blood run cold."

"Marry me," he said bluntly.

Sophie nearly fell from her chair. "W-what?"

"Will you marry me?" He stood and came round the table to take her hand and kneel at her feet. "Will you marry me, Miss Sophie Markwell? I have loved you ever so long."

Her heart felt as if it had leapt to her throat. She trembled. "I . . . I . . ."

"Say yes," he urged. "I swear I have loved you ever since you charged into my house. I know I was certain of it by the time you came crashing down from that trellis."

She knew that she was gaping, her mouth idiotically hanging open, but she couldn't stop. Marry him? This marvelous man, this prize catch, was begging to wed plain-faced Sophie Markwell?

"What can I say to convince you?" He waved toward their cats, who were lying together at the hearthside with several kittens bumbling around them. "Our cats belong together! So do we."

"Lord Breakstone . . ."

"Trevor," he corrected urgently.

"Trevor." The name sounded delightful on her lips. She repeated it in wonderment. "Trevor."

He squeezed her hand. "What is your answer, my love? And where is your father? Truly, I should have gained his permission before addressing you, dear, but I just couldn't wait."

"Papa is at the festival, along with the rest of my family. They've probably sought the nearest shelter."

A loud crack of lightning punctuated her remark.

Trevor stiffened, clenching his teeth. Sophie couldn't help reaching out to caress his cheek.

He smiled and relaxed. "What is your answer, Sophie?"

Her brows puckered in concern. "I do not know how to be a marchioness."

"Now that is a lame answer. Suffice it to say that a marchioness is primarily the wife of a marquess. I happen to think that you are eminently suitable for that role, else I'd never have fallen in love with you." He took the time to plant a soft kiss on each of her fingers. "All else will fall in place when the time comes."

The cats seemed to decide to lend their support. Rising and stretching, they padded across the room to rub against Sophie and Trevor's legs. They put forth noisy mewing and purring.

"You see?" Trevor said. "They are greatly in favor of our match."

"Yes, it seems that they are."

A door slammed shut and footsteps and voices sounded in the front hall.

"My family," Sophie announced.

"May I make one more supplication before we greet them?" Without waiting for a reply, he leaned forward and kissed her soundly.

Her heart tripled its pace. Smoothing his hair, Sophie kissed him in return. *It was right.* She belonged to him. She had long since forsaken all others.

"Yes," she whispered. "Oh, yes!"

With an unintelligible shout of happiness, he stood, lifting her up and locking her securely in his embrace.

"Surely your father will forgive me for my lack of consulting him."

She fairly chirped. "As a man of the cloth, he is full of forgiveness. Let us go to him at once!"

"Of course!"

As Sophie pulled away from the marquess, a button on her bodice caught a button on his vest. The flimsy fabric of the gown made a horrible ripping sound. Simultaneously, the kitchen door opened.

"Sophie . . ." her mother began, only to end with a gasp. "What has happened to your dress?"

"Compromised!" cried the marquess. "Again!"

Sophie felt the all-too-familiar burning blush. Her nearest shield was Lord Breakstone himself. She leapt into his arms and pressed against him.

"It was an accident," she said meekly.

"What is going on?" implored Reverend Markwell.

"Sir, I am fully prepared to marry your daughter," Trevor assured him. "In fact, I beseeched her to wed me before this unfortunate accident."

Sophie reached to the table behind him and retrieved her apron, managing to slip it over her head. She turned triumphantly. "And I said *yes!*"

"The younger generation!" The vicar shook his head. "It seems I have no say in the matter. But, Sophie, I don't even know your fiance's name!"

"Oh dear. I am remiss!" She smiled up at Trevor. "Papa, this is Lord Breakstone. You must remember my mentioning him."

"My lord." Her father stepped forward to shake Trevor's hand. "We will be pleased to have you in the family. At last," he finished in an undertone.

Trevor bowed. "Sir, I have the means and I am prepared to go to no end to make Sophie happy and comfortable."

"I am sure you will." He looked from one to the other. "When Sophie returned from London, her mother and I were deeply concerned about her state of mind. Our happy gel was suddenly sad. Now, I know that is past."

"I shall be happy forever, Papa." She took Trevor's hand and looked up into his beautiful eyes. *"Forever."*

While the rest of Sophie's family were introduced and began to celebrate the engagement, Lord Harris vaulted unseen onto the table. He looked down and mewed to Lady Jane, encouraging her to follow. When she obeyed, he led her to the cooling apple pies on one end, where they dined—thieving, stray, alley-cat fashion—in their own celebration.

ABOUT THE AUTHOR

Cathleen Clare lives with her family in Ironton, Ohio. She is the author of nine regency romances, including AN ELUSIVE GROOM, LORD SCANDAL'S LADY, A PRICELESS ACQUISITION, and LORD MONTJOY'S COUNTRY INN. Cathleen is currently working on her next Zebra regency romance, A FAMILY AFFAIR, which will be published in May 1999. Cathleen loves hearing from her readers and you may write to her c/o Zebra Books. Please include a self-addressed stamped envelope if you wish a response.

WATCH FOR THESE REGENCY ROMANCES

BREACH OF HONOR   (0-8217-5111-5, $4.50)
by Phylis Warady

DeLACEY'S ANGEL   (0-8217-4978-1, $3.99)
by Monique Ellis

A DECEPTIVE BEQUEST   (0-8217-5380-0, $4.50)
by Olivia Sumner

A RAKE'S FOLLY   (0-8217-5007-0, $3.99)
by Claudette Williams

AN INDEPENDENT LADY   (0-8217-3347-8, $3.95)
by Lois Stewart

Available wherever paperbacks are sold, or order direct from the Publisher. Send cover price plus 50¢ per copy for mailing and handling to Kensington Publishing Corp., Consumer Orders, or call (toll free) 888-345-BOOK, to place your order using Mastercard or Visa. Residents of New York and Tennessee must include sales tax. DO NOT SEND CASH.

LOOK FOR THESE REGENCY ROMANCES

SCANDAL'S DAUGHTER   (0-8217-5273-1, $4.50)
by Carola Dunn

A DANGEROUS AFFAIR   (0-8217-5294-4, $4.50)
by Mona Gedney

A SUMMER COURTSHIP   (0-8217-5358-4, $4.50)
by Valerie King

TIME'S TAPESTRY   (0-8217-5381-9, $4.99)
by Joan Overfield

LADY STEPHANIE   (0-8217-5341-X, $4.50)
by Jeanne Savery

Available wherever paperbacks are sold, or order direct from the Publisher. Send cover price plus 50¢ per copy for mailing and handling to Kensington Publishing Corp., Consumer Orders, or call (toll free) 888-345-BOOK, to place your order using Mastercard or Visa. Residents of New York and Tennessee must include sales tax. DO NOT SEND CASH.